DUDE!

Stories and Stuff
for Boys

DUDE!

Stories and Stuff
for Boys

Edited by Sandy Asher
and David L. Harrison

DUTTON CHILDREN'S BOOKS

DUTTON CHILDREN'S BOOKS

A division of Penguin Young Readers Group

Published by the Penguin Group

Penguin Group (USA) Inc., 375 Hudson Street, New York, New York 10014, U.S.A. • Penguin Group (Canada), 90 Eglinton Avenue East, Suite 700, Toronto, Ontario, Canada M4P 2Y3 (a division of Pearson Penguin Canada Inc.) • Penguin Books Ltd, 80 Strand, London WC2R 0RL, England • Penguin Ireland, 25 St Stephen's Green, Dublin 2, Ireland (a division of Penguin Books Ltd) • Penguin Group (Australia), 250 Camberwell Road, Camberwell, Victoria 3124, Australia (a division of Pearson Australia Group Pty Ltd) • Penguin Books India Pvt Ltd, 11 Community Centre, Panchsheel Park, New Delhi - 110 017, India • Penguin Group (NZ), Cnr Airborne and Rosedale Roads, Albany, Auckland 1310, New Zealand (a division of Pearson New Zealand Ltd) • Penguin Books (South Africa) (Pty) Ltd, 24 Sturdee Avenue, Rosebank, Johannesburg 2196, South Africa • Penguin Books Ltd, Registered Offices: 80 Strand, London WC2R 0RL, England

CIP Data is available.

Published in the United States by Dutton Children's Books,
a division of Penguin Young Readers Group
345 Hudson Street, New York, New York 10014
www.penguin.com/youngreaders

Designed by Jason Henry
Printed in USA • First Edition
ISBN 0-525-47684-9
1 3 5 7 9 10 8 6 4 2

To the founders and organizers of the Children's Literature Festival, Warrensburg, MO, and the Children's Literature Festival of the Ozarks, Springfield, MO—with years and miles and tons of gratitude

—S.A.

To Eugene and JoAnn Kennon with love

—D.L.H.

CONTENTS

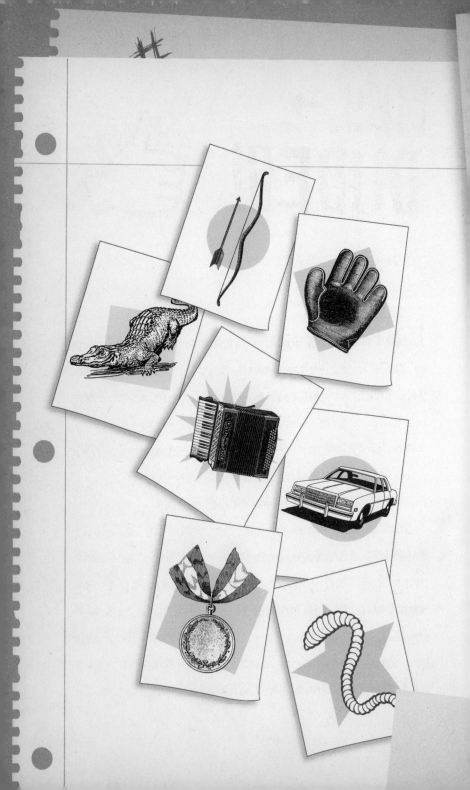

HEY, →
DUDES!

Hi! If you're a boy, this book is for you. Everything in *Dude!* was written with boys in mind—stories, poems, plays, and real boyhood adventures remembered by some of your favorite writers.

You can read it, too, girls. In fact, grown-up girls wrote some of the neat stuff you'll find in here.

But it's all neat stuff for and about *boys*.

Somewhere between playing with toy cars and dreaming of real ones, boys stop being "little" and start being "big." You guys know what we're talking about. Right? You change, not all at once but by a series of small steps. It's hard to say how many steps there are. One day you're just not a kid anymore. You're a young man. You're different. You're treated differently, too.

And your world fills up with questions, sometimes when you least expect them: Can I? Will I? Should I? When? Why? How?

Do I have to?

Do I dare?

You need answers. So do the characters in this book. They face the tough challenges of growing up: taunting classmates, teasing brothers, tests of courage, cunning villains, the violence of war, and violence in the street. They struggle, they scramble, they stretch. And once in a while, they laugh! Some of them find what they're searching for; some don't—at least not yet. But one thing's sure: *they never give up.*

As authors, we visit schools every year, and we meet a lot of boys. Some of your faces stick with us for a long time afterward, maybe forever: the kids who laugh at our jokes, the ones who listen closely because they want to become writers, too, and especially all the boys who ask, "Will you make a book just for us?"

Yup. This is it, fellas.

We were young once, too. We remember times when we wondered if anyone else on the planet had questions like ours. Thinking about those times when we needed answers gave us the idea for this book. We reached out to writers across the country. We asked them to help us create a book for guys. They could write a poem, a play, a true story, or fiction...we didn't care as long as it was all about boys.

Our mailboxes began filling up with fantastic writing. That didn't surprise us. We only invited superior writers—every one a prizewinner—to participate.

So read on! You'll meet superheroes, soldiers, farmers, alien "bots," big brothers, little brothers, angels, a wayward baseball, a friendly worm, and a very heavy accordion! We think you'll like them all.

We want you to know that we made this book in your honor. Every writer in here told us how much he or she appreciated the opportunity to talk to you and to hold up a light to brighten the path you're on.

Being a boy is special, but it's not easy. Here are some friends who are all rooting for *you*!

Sandy Asher
David L. Harrison

DUDE!

Stories and Stuff
for Boys

THE TOWER

BY Sneed B. Collard III

The first time I stepped onto the dock and looked across the smooth surface of Wakulla Springs, I felt I'd stepped into the age of dinosaurs. On the far bank, Spanish moss dripped from ancient cypress trees that had probably scratched the backs of tyrannosaurs. Strange birds, like pterodactyls, perched with their wings spread out in mysterious rituals. On nearby logs, turtles stacked up on one another's backs like prehistoric dominoes. But as my eyes swiveled across the scene, it wasn't the trees or the birds or the turtles that pegged my attention.

It was the tower. The tower at the far end of the beach. The one with the three platforms, painted red, white, and blue, each rising higher than the last. The one with the rickety rusting frame and kids flinging themselves like human sacrifices off the top, toward the springs below.

Watching those kids jump and shout and scream, I knew. That tower was not going to let me escape this place. Already, its creaking, iron beams were taunting me, whispering, "So you're here at last. What are you going to do? Do you really think you can beat me?"

It was the summer I turned eleven years old, my third year doing the divorce shuffle. A few months earlier, my dad had landed a job as an assistant biology professor at the University of West Florida, and I flew to Pensacola in June, two days after school let out. As I nervously walked down the jetway, I spotted my dad waiting for me. He wore his usual T-shirt and faded jeans riddled with holes from acid splashed in his laboratory.

He scooped me up in a hug that popped my ribs and squeezed the air from my lungs.

"Ugh!" I grunted, but I didn't mind.

His crushing hug told me that we were still a family. That despite everything, he still loved me.

It didn't take long for me to discover that I liked Florida. Yeah, there were a few scary rednecks driving around with shotguns, and the mosquitoes drank my blood like it was Coca-Cola, but the Sunshine State had good things, too. The Gulf of Mexico, for instance, with its bathtub-warm water and blinding-white sand beaches. And the lightning storms that exploded overhead like atom bombs every afternoon. And the things that revved me up more than anything—what my dad called the Long Green Bumpy Things.

Alligators.

Today, of course, alligators are as common as fire ants, but this was back in the 1970s, before the gators made their great comeback. A few survived deep in swamps, but I'd never seen a wild one and didn't know anyone who had. Before flying to Florida, I'd made my dad promise me that no matter what, we would track one down. I wasted no time holding him to his word.

"Dad, when are we going to go see an alligator?"

"Soon, son. I've got a lot of work this week, but we can go after that."

"Dad, you *promised* we would go see an alligator."

"I know. I know. We will. Just be patient."

I wasn't. I pestered him without mercy.

Finally, one day in July, he told me, "Okay. Pack your bags. We're going somewhere that has more gators than you have zits."

The following Friday, my dad, my stepmother, Penny, and I squeezed onto the bench seat of Big Red—our '57 pickup with the bald tires and a tailgate held on by bungee cords. My dad drove east but wouldn't tell me where we were going. Every time I asked, he said, "You'll see."

"But there are alligators there, right?" I asked.

"Gazillions."

"Hmm," I said, settling back, unconvinced, against the cracked vinyl seat of our truck.

We took the old highway that followed the Gulf Coast, past the swimming pool waters of Destin and Panama City Beach. Then we turned inland and drove through endless plantations of pine trees. After three hours, my dad flicked on Big Red's blinker and we turned right, at a sign that read

WELCOME TO WAKULLA SPRINGS RESORT

AND EDWARD BALL WILDLIFE SANCTUARY

I bolted upright. "Is this it? Are we here?"

My dad grinned. "Yep."

We parked in front of a huge whitewashed hotel with arching doorways and a Spanish-tile roof. We checked in and left our bags in our room, and then bought tickets for a "jungle boat" ride. I practically ran toward the dock. Finally, I was going to see a real alligator!

When I reached the dock, though, my sandals skidded to a halt. It wasn't because I saw alligators. Instead, my eyes riveted in on that enormous rusting iron-and-wood hulk rising from the far end of the beach.

The tower.

"Look at those kids jumping from those platforms," my stepmother, Penny, said, following my gaze. "That has to be dangerous. Why would anyone do something so crazy?"

My dad and I looked at each other, our thoughts the same: *She just doesn't get it.*

And instantly, I could feel the tower sending its tendrils deep into my brain, daring me, challenging me to put my courage on the line.

* * *

But for now, we had gators to see. Wakulla Springs pumped out so much water that it formed a river called the Wakulla River that ran a dozen miles to the Gulf of Mexico. Leaving the dock, the jungle boat headed downstream into a world I could never have imagined. Massive alligators—gray, it turned out, not green—lay lazily along the banks or in rafts of lily pads in the river. The gators lay so still that when my dad said, "Those are just fake alligators for the tourists," I at first believed him.

Then, an eight-footer suddenly slipped off a log into the sparkling, clear water. My jaw dropped and I punched my dad in the shoulder. He just grinned.

And the gators were just part of it. Turtles and snakes filled every log and tree branch. Those ptero-dactyl birds—which were called "water turkeys" or anhingas—dived under our boat for meals of mullet and other fish. A bald eagle soared overhead, the first I'd ever seen.

After the jungle cruise finished, we changed into our swimsuits and headed back down to the beach. My dad and I strapped on our masks and snorkels and waded into the chilly water. I have to admit I felt a little nervous, especially when two bull alligators began bellowing from the opposite shore, only a hundred yards away. No one else seemed concerned, however. Apparently, the gators knew which side of the springs they were supposed to stay on, and the people did, too.

We kicked out from the beach twenty or thirty yards and then turned left toward the main springs. The sandy bottom lay only five or six feet below us, but as we swam farther, it dropped down to ten, fifteen, twenty feet deep. Then my stomach trampolined as I saw a deep dark hole open into the bowels of the earth—the main springs.

Grinning, my dad turned back to me and motioned me forward. We paddled out a few more yards, and suddenly I stared straight down into nothing. But it wasn't nothing, I soon realized. Shafts of sunlight reached down into the springs, and as my eyes adjusted, I began to make out dim, dark details of logs and sand shimmering two hundred feet below. Gawking down at them, I half expected to plunge into oblivion, but the upwelling water kept me afloat.

As I turned and began paddling toward shore, however, I heard a giant splash close by. Thinking it was an alligator about to sink its teeth into me, I jerked my head out of the water. What I saw was more menacing than any alligator. It was the tower looming almost directly above me. From below, its ancient frame looked even more ominous than it had from down the beach. It was only three stories tall, but from down in the water, it looked ten or twelve, easy. As three teenage boys launched off the top level, a chill made my body twitch. It might have been from the cool water, but I didn't think so.

When we staggered to shore, dripping wet, my dad turned to me. "Was that great or was that great?"

I blew a plug of snot from my nose and nodded.

"You want to go check out the tower?"

"I'm hungry," I said.

My dad's eyes met mine for a moment. Then he said, "Okay. Let's go eat."

After dinner, the air began to cool and we all again walked down to the water. By now, the swimmers and tower-jumpers had surrendered the springs to the wildlife. We strolled along the deserted beach and, before we knew it, found ourselves at the narrow boardwalk leading to the tower.

"Let's climb up," Penny suggested.

I went ahead, my sandals flapping against the wooden planks of the walk. I stopped on the first level—the red level.

This isn't so bad. Must only be eight feet above the water. I've done that plenty of times.

Penny and my dad passed me, though, and began climbing the ancient stairs up to the second level. My heart picking up speed, I followed. When I reached the white platform, I at first thought, *Hmm. This isn't much higher than the red platform.* As I looked over the rail, though, my legs began to shake. It's not that it was so high—only twenty or so feet up—but that it was high *if you planned to jump.*

"What a view," Penny said, admiring the pink glow of sunset reflecting off a distant thunderhead. "This is great up here. Let's keep going."

She and my dad hurried up to the blue level, the top platform, and, hands sweating, I trailed behind. When I emerged onto the top, dread hit me like a body blow.

Here, no protective roof reached over me, just raw,

open sky. Clutching the iron railing, I looked down and felt the world wobble under me. Never in my life had I stood so high and actually imagined jumping off. Yeah, we were only thirty-five feet up, but it might have been a thousand. The surface of the springs silently swirled far below, as if I were looking at it from an airplane. I spotted the dim shapes of six-foot-long fish called alligator gars floating in the water and thought, *How many skeletons of children lie beneath them?*

Penny sighed. "Oh, this is lovely. I could stay up here forever."

My father looked at me. "What do you think, son?"

I met his eyes and knew for the first time that he understood what I was facing. I shrugged. "I don't know."

"You'd have to be a fool to jump off," he offered.

I nodded, but we both knew that that was the whole point.

I asked, "Would you do it?"

He laughed. "Are you kidding? Not a chance."

I knew he was lying.

I'll bet when he was my age, he would have been the first one off the top.

"Let's go back to the hotel lobby and play hearts," Penny suggested.

She didn't have to ask twice.

The next morning after breakfast, we took the glass-bottomed-boat ride around the springs and then returned to the beach. My dad and I again snorkeled, and afterward I lay down on a towel, letting the tropical sun suck the drops of water one by one from my skin. Soon drops of sweat replaced them. Nearby, my dad was reading a thick paperback and Penny, a magazine. I sat up and gazed at the tower.

"Wait as long as you want," it murmured. "You can't put it off forever."

I stood up and said, "I'll be back."

My dad glanced at me and nodded. His eyes said, "Do what you gotta do."

I began walking up the beach, the arguments already ricocheting inside my skull.

You don't have to do this. Just jump off the red platform, the lowest one. You don't have anything to prove. You're as brave as the next kid. Just take a couple of quick dives and forget about it.

Yeah, right.

By the time I reached the wooden walkway to the tower, a few families with their kids milled around. Some jumped off the red—or lowest—platform, and a few had climbed up to the white and blue platforms, but no one was jumping off. Yet.

I twirled my arms to loosen up and then walked to the edge of the red platform. I took a breath, then dived. The cool rush of the seventy-two-degree liquid felt good against my skin. I opened my eyes underwater to see plants swaying on the bottom and the tower's iron supports reaching down like rusting roots into the sand. I kicked to the surface, blinked, and looked up. In full sunlight, the tower didn't seem nearly as ominous as it had the afternoon before.

What was I so afraid of?

Feeling cocky, I climbed the ladder and did several more dives off the red platform. I even did a backflip.

This is easy.

With a surge of energy, I again climbed the ladder and hopped up the steps to the white platform, the second level. I walked out to the edge of the platform, looked down, and...

My mouth filled with chalk.

The surface of the water sparkled in the sunlight, but it wasn't an inch closer than it had been the night before. If anything, it looked farther away.

What was I thinking—that the tower would somehow get shorter during the night?

I clutched the safety rail and backed away from the edge. Heart hammering, I rested my elbows on the rail and pretended to admire the view. Two other boys, perhaps a year younger than I was, came up and also peered over the edge.

"Man, that's high," one said. "You gonna jump?"

"No way," said the other. "Didn't you hear about the kid last summer? They say he dove off the top and landed wrong."

"Did he die?"

"No, he broke his back and is totally paralyzed. He can't even go to the bathroom by himself."

The other one made a face and said "Ugh!" Then they disappeared back down the stairs.

I let out a breath, relieved they hadn't jumped. Then I returned to the edge and stared down. Nerves fired up and down my body as I clutched the rusty rail. Several more kids and an adult walked by, mostly headed for the top level. I let them pass. After fifteen minutes, disgusted with myself, I stomped back down the steps and dived off the red platform. Splashing angrily, I sprinted back to the beach, waded onto shore, and flopped down on my towel.

My dad looked up from his book. "How'd it go?"

I avoided his eyes. "Okay."

Suddenly I heard a loud rebel yell and looked up in time to see a body fling itself off the tower's top level. A knot twisted inside of me.

The teenagers had arrived.

After lunch, we took a short siesta in our room and then headed back toward the beach. I stalked ahead, by now furious with myself for being such a coward. While my dad and Penny went snorkeling, I marched directly to the tower. I dived off the lowest level once and then climbed straight up to the white platform.

The tower swarmed with kids. A few looked like me—pale, visitors from somewhere else. Most, though, had brown skin and bleached hair and called one another by name using accents straight out of a Civil War movie. Some were older—teenagers—but not all. I watched with embarrassment as a group of eight- or nine-year-olds climbed to the top platform. Moments later, I heard them scream like warriors as their bodies hurtled past me into the water below. Then I saw two local girls take the plunge.

That's it, I scolded myself. *No more messing around.*

Still touching the rail, I walked to the edge of the white platform and looked down.

Go! I commanded myself.

My legs stayed put.

I sucked in my breath and lifted my right foot out over the void and said to myself, *Now just keep going. Push off with your left foot, and it will all be over.* Of course, that's when my left leg began jackhammering so badly, I had to step back from the edge altogether.

I kept daring myself like that, scolding myself, using a thousand tricks to get myself to jump. I don't know how long it went on. Maybe ten minutes. Maybe thirty. Dozens of kids ran past me, some leaping off the white platform, most heading to the blue level above. I could hardly believe what they were doing. Some just jumped, but others did cannonballs and back and front flips. A few—the bravest—dived headfirst, their muscular brown bodies plunging in graceful arcs until they torpedoed through the water's surface. They were the gods of Wakulla Springs. I could see it in their faces as they walked back up. They didn't bother to throw a glance my way. I was the lowest scum in the kingdom.

And yet still I cowered there, my feet screwed to the wood, clutching the iron railing like it was the one thing that stood between me and death. My dad and Penny finished their swim and returned to the beach. A bull alligator roared from across the springs. Countless times, I psyched myself up and even bent my knees to jump, but they didn't move. I simply could not will myself to step off of that platform.

I was about to slither away in defeat when the chubby, middle-aged man joined me. It was during a lull in activity, when everyone else was either above or below and I had the entire white platform to myself. Up the stairs the man clomped. He had a round, flabby face and wore baggy white swim trunks that looked like boxer shorts. His raw sunburned skin proved that he, too, was a newcomer.

"Hi," I said.

"Hello," he said, catching his breath. Then he cautiously peered over the edge. "It's a long way down, isn't it?"

I nodded. "Have you jumped off before?"

"No. This is my first time this way."

We said nothing for a moment. Then he asked, "You jumped before?"

"No. It's my first time, too."

We both stood staring down, watching the bodies of the locals thudding like cement sacks as they hit the water. The man pretended to look around at the scenery for a few minutes, but it didn't fool me. I'd played that game myself. Finally, he shook his head and stepped back. "Well, see you—"

"Wait!" I blurted.

He stopped and our eyes met.

"I tell you what," I told him. "I'll go off and then you can go off after me."

The man regarded me for a moment, then stared back down at the water. I could tell he had his doubts. Worse, he didn't seem to *need* to do this. Not like I did.

Finally, he said, "I guess we could do that."

I immediately wanted to take back my words.

You idiot! Now you have to go off.

But that was the problem. I *didn't* have to go off. Suddenly I thought about the time Mike Leva had challenged me to a fight and I'd never showed up. Or the time my friends had dared me to tell Susan Hendrickson I liked her and I'd chickened out. Each time something like that had happened, I'd lost something. Each time, my hopes for ever turning into a real man had wilted just a little bit more.

This is going to be another one of those failures.

The man with the white bathing suit still looked at me, and I wondered if he'd ever chickened out.

I'll bet he has. Maybe that's just how life is. Some things you chicken out on. Since everyone else is chickening out, too, it's okay.

But then I thought of my dad. He wasn't that way. The kids above me weren't. And right then, I decided I didn't want to be that way, either.

My knees stopped quivering, and I stepped forward. Then I took a deep breath and leaped. For a moment, I hung there, my chest filled with terror, but my mind empty. Then, in a flash, the gravity of the springs sucked me down, faster, faster—*PWSHHHH!*

I hit the surface and was under. Water shot up my nose, and my testicles throbbed because I hadn't kept my feet together. I didn't care. I opened my eyes to see the aquarium world of the springs all around me. Bubbles. Fish. Sunken logs. Then I was back on the surface, adrenaline pounding through me, blinking up at the man who'd been standing next to me. I grinned and waved. He waved back and also leaped, making a loud splash fifteen feet from me. A second later, he bobbed to the surface. We looked at each other.

"Good jump," I told him.

"You, too."

I kicked my legs and swam all the way in to the beach.

That night, I tossed in my hotel bed, replaying the jump. Each time I leaped in my head, my whole body jerked, reliving every sensation, from the weightlessness to the quick fall toward the water to the impact of hitting the surface. I felt good lying there. Proud of what I'd done. After an hour or so, however, while my dad and Penny snored in the bed next to me, I again began to hear the call.

"You tell yourself it's over," the tower whispered, "but both of us know it's not. You're barely halfway there. You don't leave until noon tomorrow. I'll be waiting—if you've got the balls."

* * *

The next morning, we packed our suitcases and put on our swimsuits for one last visit to the beach. My dad and I again snorkeled and then I walked to the tower for the last time. I didn't bother warming up by diving off the red platform. Instead, I climbed straight up to the top level and looked over the edge.

I took a deep breath and, without hesitating, made one glorious, courageous leap into the springs far below.

Well, maybe in my fantasies.

What really happened is that I looked down from the top platform and felt my knees tremble all over again. And I decided I'd had enough. Yeah, I'd only gotten halfway there, but at least I'd gone that far. I let myself feel good about that for a moment. Then I climbed back down the tower. Walking toward my dad and Penny, I took one last look back at the rusting giant perched over the deepest part of the springs.

The tower chuckled and said, "That's it. Run. Run all the way back to California. But don't forget, I'll still be waiting for you next year."

I whispered, "I know. But next year, you'll have to worry about *me*, too."

THE SQUIDS

BY Walter Simonson

Ben Bogdanove felt the drop of sweat reach the end of his nose and hang there. He was sure that if it fell, the sound it made as it hit the floor would echo through the deserted mall and alert the security guards. He could see their shadows moving across the dimly lit storefront windows along the promenade off to his left. He pressed himself against the back of the little kiosk, trying to merge with the darkness.

If the guards caught him in the mall hours after closing, he was doomed. No amount of explaining would convince them, or worse, his parents, that what he was doing was saving them all from a fate worse than death! And if he was right—he knew he WAS right—the uniformed guards were really bots already! No longer human except in outward appearance. Forget his parents. If the bots caught him, he'd be lucky if he ever saw his parents again!

Because Ben knew a secret. A terrible secret.

He'd known it for a whole week now, ever since the day his mother had taken him to the Big Mall to get new clothes for school. Ben was only eleven, but he was already starting to grow, to shoot up early like his four brothers before him. Because his birthday fell right at the beginning of the school year, he always got clothes for presents. Which pretty much sucked.

Now, as Ben hunkered down behind the kiosk trying not to breathe, he realized that if it hadn't been for that back-to-school shopping trip to the mall, he'd never have discovered that the aliens were here. That the invasion of Earth, predicted in practically every science fiction movie since the dawn of time, had already begun.

And nobody knew it but him!

Ben's mom had let him check out the latest video-game releases at the TwitchBoy store while she went to look for another food processor. Their food processors were always breaking. Ben had been heading for the store when he saw it: a new freestanding display set up in front of the playground-equipment store. Two pretty young women and a young man were manning the kiosk. Three easy chairs were lined up in a row beside it. HEAD-EAZE read the sign above them. *Tired? Beat? Worn-out from Shopping? Let Us Relax and Reenergize You! You Won't Believe How You Feel! Stop by Right Now!* Ben stood openmouthed at the sight. It looked like the salespeople were holding mechanical squids!

Cool!

As he was about to walk over for a closer inspection, he saw one of the pretty women smile and stop a tired-looking man lugging several shopping bags. Ben couldn't hear what she was saying, but the man nodded and, setting down his bags, sat in one of the chairs. The woman moved behind him. She flipped a switch on the bottom of the squid, and its tentacles began to vibrate! Then, before Ben's astonished eyes, the woman brought the tips of those tentacles down onto the man's scalp.

The man gave a brief start, then relaxed as the woman ran the tentacles all around the top of his head. Watching closely, Ben realized the mechanical squid's body was really a handle. Flaring out from the end above the woman's hand were a set of copper-colored metal tines like tentacles, each about a foot long and slightly bent in at the ends. They vibrated gently as they moved across the man's head.

Then, to Ben's horror, the man's eyes rolled back until only the whites were showing. Ben caught his breath and ducked back behind a pillar, suddenly not wanting to be noticed. The man's mouth hung open, and his head lolled slightly from side to side as the squid's tentacles continued to crawl across his scalp. Ben could see the kiosk shelves were lined with rows of the things nesting in charging cradles. Just like his parents' cell phone, the squids must be electrically powered with rechargeable batteries.

The woman finished. She clicked the squid into an empty cradle and the guy just sat there, his face blank. Then she touched his shoulder. He blinked once, twice, and stood up suddenly. Stretching his neck from side to side, he turned and spoke a few words to the woman, then headed off into the mall, ramrod straight, taking long purposeful strides as he disappeared into the crowd. Next to the chair sat his shopping bags, abandoned. Ben watched with unblinking eyes as the woman slipped them behind the kiosk. He saw with surprise that several other shopping bags were already sitting there in the shadows. Why would shoppers simply abandon their shopping bags like that?

In a flash, Ben had the answer. The squid was some kind of brain transfuser, draining the human minds of their humanity and filling them with alien thoughts. With an alien consciousness. An alien who had no use for their shopping bags or their contents! A man had walked up to the booth; an alien had walked away. The attendants were aliens in human guise, and the squids were their weapons of conquest!

Ben was an expert on aliens. He'd seen almost every movie and TV show ever made about them. Knew how they thought, knew what they were planning, knew where they were going to strike. It was mostly America, but sometimes Tokyo. Almost always, they targeted the big cities, not suburban communities with their malls and their rows of nearly identical houses. These aliens were clearly smarter than most of the aliens he'd seen in the movies. These guys were attacking America where they were least expected.

When he got home from the mall, Ben surfed the Web using his brother's iMac while Billy was visiting his girlfriend. A quick Google search confirmed his worst fears. Head-Eaze had kiosks at six different malls in the greater Chicago area, but they were a brand-new business. The aliens couldn't have altered too many humans yet.

The drop of sweat at the tip of his nose fell. It hit the concrete floor with a plop he could barely hear...but he was certain that four storefronts away, the nearest shadow froze instantly. Desperately, Ben held his breath and closed his eyes tight, as if somehow, not seeing things made him harder to see as well.

Ben was wearing his darkest blue jeans and a ratty deep blue pullover. He'd used his dad's shoe polish to blacken his oldest pair of sneakers. He'd borrowed his sister's belly pack to carry some of Dad's tools, including a flashlight, screwdrivers, and a wire stripper. He'd even taken Ted's sports eyeblack. His brother painted the stuff under his eyes when he played baseball to cut down on glare, but Ben had smeared his entire face with it, commando-style. He knew that blending into the dark was crucial to the success of his mission. He also knew that every member of his family would kill him if they found out he'd borrowed their stuff without asking.

Ben's brothers didn't know anything about aliens. They were all jocks who played on school sports teams and brought home gold trophies. Just like their father had done. His brothers teased Ben, laughing that he couldn't have caught a football with both hands covered in Super Glue! It was true. He wasn't coordinated like they were.

But Ben had found his hands were good at small things. Big Ben, their father, was an electrician. He had a complete workshop in the basement, and Ben spent hours there, watching his dad take broken things apart and put them back together, fixed. With Big Ben's encouragement, he'd even begun helping out, learning about live wires and grounds and circuit diagrams. There was still a lot he didn't know, but he was a quick student, always had been. He might not win any trophies at school, but he knew how to deal with aliens!

He risked a peek around the corner of the kiosk. The shadow was no closer, but it hadn't moved either. He wondered if security bots could stand in one spot for hours. He couldn't. He had to get back into hiding before the mall opened in the morning. His parents thought he was spending the night with his best friend, Matt. The two were blood brothers—they'd spit in their palms, gripped hands, and sworn friendship with all the bad words they knew. So Ben had told Matt his plan. And they both knew there wasn't an adult anywhere who would have believed Ben.

Matt had been dying to go with him. But Ben shook his head. It was too risky for both of them to be away from home for a night. Besides, if Ben didn't come back, well, somebody was going to have to tell their parents. Matt protested that it was less dangerous to go to the mall overnight than tell their parents, but Ben was firm. He'd seen too many movies where some knuckle-head went off to find the alien hive without telling anybody where he was going and never came back and nobody ever knew what happened to him. So right after supper, they'd ridden their bikes together to the mall to see *Invaders from Mars II*. Then Matt went home. Alone.

Now Ben's bike was locked in the bike rack outside the west entrance to the mall. His school clothes were in his old knapsack beneath the garbage bag in the lit-ter can in the men's room on the first floor. In the morning, with a little luck, he could be out the mall doors seconds after they were opened and still get to school only a few minutes late. Nobody would have missed him. Nobody ever paid any attention to him anyway. He'd just slip into old Miss Trattorinni's class, and she'd mark him present. That wouldn't be a problem.

But now…now was a problem.

He risked another peek down the darkened mall.

The shadows were moving, gliding smoothly toward the other end of the mall. This was it! Time to move.

Ben stretched out full-length on the floor and reached carefully under the kiosk, feeling around. The electrical cable that powered the charging cradles had to be plugged into an outlet somewhere in the floor. A moment later, his fingers wrapped around the plug. Carefully, he tugged on it.

Nothing happened. He tugged harder. Still nothing.

This was bad. He had to get his hands on the plug or his plan was dead in the water.

He took off the belly pack, lay on his stomach, and gripped the plug with both hands. Gritting his teeth, he gave a sharp jerk upward. The plug came free, but there was a soft thump as the cable struck the bottom of the kiosk. Ben looked around wildly, waiting for the security bots to come charging out of the darkness.

There was only silence. He let out his breath slowly and pulled the plug and cable out from under the kiosk. Another glance around told him that the shadows had not returned.

Ben crouched between the end of the kiosk and the wall behind him. He took a tiny flashlight out of the belly pack, put it between his teeth, and turned it on, aiming the beam at the plug and cable in his hand.

His eye caught a flicker of movement off in the darkness to his right. He killed the light and, pulling the cable with him, squeezed under the kiosk on his stomach. Its metal bottom pressed hard against his back.

Then, as he peered out from beneath his hiding place, he nearly gasped aloud. His belly pack! It was sitting on the floor in the shadows just beyond the edge of the kiosk. Before he could grab it, a dark shape glided across the floor toward him. A moment later, a shoe—a black shoe with thick soft soles—planted itself silently on the floor a mere eighteen inches from his face. Just as silently, another shoe joined it.

Ben held his breath. He could see the slight hump of the belly pack in the deep shadow. Any moment the security bot would look down and see it! The weight of the kiosk seemed to be squeezing him into the concrete floor. He felt dizzy. He was sweating again.

Did eleven-year-olds ever have heart attacks? What would they think when they found his bike outside the mall tomorrow? Would Matt be able to convince his parents of what had really happened?

Thirty seconds went by. Ben knew he was going to have to breathe or die. As silently as he could, he opened his mouth wide and exhaled, trying not to gasp. The right shoe moved a fraction, the side of the sole almost touching the belly pack's strap. Ben suppressed the urge to run for it. He wouldn't have a chance.

He felt like crying. The aliens were going to win, and no one would ever know what had happened to the stupid kid with the wire-rim glasses and chipped front tooth. Briefly, he thought of the bicycle accident where he'd slammed into the parked car and sailed over the handlebars right into the trunk, teeth first. He squeezed his eyes tight in despair. Now, he thought, he'd never ride his bike again or—

He opened his eyes. The feet were gone!

Ben looked around as fast as his stiff neck would allow.

Nothing! No movement anywhere. He began to reach out from under the kiosk for his belly pack. And froze. In his mind's eye, he saw the shadow, cunning, malevolent, infinitely patient, perched silently on top of the kiosk, waiting for him to make the first move. Just what an alien would do. Ben pulled his arm back, squinted at his watch, squeezing the button on the right side of its face with his other hand. The dial lit briefly: 12:35 A.M. He prayed the thing wouldn't sit up there all night!

But Ben knew aliens, knew them intimately. And he knew, as surely as he was lying there getting more uncomfortable by the minute, that any alien worth its salt would wait for an eternity if it meant enslaving or killing one more human being. He'd have to grit it out.

The sixth time he checked his watch, it was after 1:00 A.M. He hadn't heard a sound in all that time. Surely he would have felt the bot climbing onto the shelves. His belly pack was tantalizingly close, and it wouldn't take him five minutes to fix the plug. The silence was total. The aliens had probably gone to the other end of the mall, and if he were ever going to do this, he had to get started. His shoulders were starting to cramp in the confined space and he was scared. Much more scared than he'd been hiding under the backseats in the movie plex, Theater 17, waiting for the mall to close.

His fingers had just begun to reach out for the belly pack when there was a soft thud on the other side of the kiosk. Ben bit his tongue, waiting for an alien hand to haul him out to his doom. But there was only silence. When he finally dared twist his head to the right, he saw a shadow with what might have been soft-soled shoes disappearing down the great hall between the storefronts, heading for the mall's north wing.

Idiot! Of course he hadn't felt the thing leap to the top of the kiosk. Any aliens worth their salt used anti-gravity!

There was no time to lose.

His hand snaked out and grabbed the belly pack. He pushed himself out from under the kiosk and crouched between it and the wall. A moment later, Ben had his flashlight on and was studying the plug at the end of the kiosk's power cable. Perfect! Just as he'd hoped, it was a polarized add-on plug!

It had three heavy prongs sticking out of it. Two

were flat and parallel, one a little larger than the other. And right below them was a round-centered prong, the ground. A lot of ordinary appliances had molded plugs that were part of the cord; the only way to remove them was to cut them off. But Ben knew that heavier electrical cables often had add-on plugs attached to them, large plugs that were installed separately, with the cable's wires screwed into terminals inside the plug. He pulled a Phillips-head screwdriver out of the belly pack and set to work taking the plug apart.

In less than a minute, he had disconnected the cable's red live wire and white neutral wire from the plug's terminals. Then Ben reconnected each wire to the opposing terminal within the plug. The connections secure, he snapped the plug together and screwed it back onto the end of the cable. The plug looked completely normal, but inside, the two electrical wires were now reversed. He'd done it. He'd completed the traditional maneuver for defeating aliens.

Ben lay down, feeling around for the floor receptacle. Carefully, he lined up the plug and drove it home into the socket. A quick look told him the hall was still empty of bots.

The men's room on the first level was unlocked, and

he slipped into it quietly. The smell of fresh disinfectant signaled that it had already been cleaned; it would remain empty till morning. He retrieved his knapsack. He'd seen no more shadows. All he had to do now was wait until the mall opened in the morning. Very quietly, he moistened a handful of toilet paper and began wiping the eyeblack off his face.

After school the next day, Ben stopped by the mall on his way home. He had scarcely been able to keep his eyes open during class, and he desperately wanted to get home to sleep. But he had to know.

Nonchalantly, Ben strolled down the center of the mall, trying to stay inconspicuous. There it was up ahead! The Head-Eaze kiosk! A woman was just sitting down in a chair. With a flourish, the handsome guy attendant brought the "squid" down onto her head. Ben watched her closely under lowered eyelids as he walked slowly past. One of the other attendants glanced in his direction, and Ben forced his eyes to look at the windows of the Great Playground store behind the kiosk. Just one more kid looking at the giant jungle gyms in the window. She turned away toward another potential victim.

But Ben had seen what he'd needed to see. The woman in the easy chair was almost done. Her eyes were half-closed but they were still alert. They hadn't rolled back; her head wasn't lolling from side to side. The squids were useless!

The woman got up, thanked the attendant, picked up her shopping bag, and walked away. She was slightly stooped from her load, but her head moved back and forth, looking at the store windows as she passed. She was still herself. The guy watched her go, one eyebrow raised.

Ben slumped against the back of the pillar for a moment and grinned. Then he headed for the mall exit and home. It had worked, just as he knew it would! It was the one surefire method he knew for defeating aliens, shown in movie after movie. He'd accessed the alien equipment and reversed its polarity. Ben knew that reversing the polarity was bad for a lot of earth appliances; it was obviously death on alien gizmos. That's why every guy who flew in a spaceship knew the trick. Ben felt just like Geordi from *Star Trek: The Next Generation*. Or Lancelot Williamson in *The Great Saucer Attack*. Or any one of hundreds of other heroes who'd reversed polarity and saved the day when it turned out that alien machines couldn't handle electricity turned inside out. The squids would no longer work properly. Just let those creeps try to operate their brain transfusers now!

But as he swung onto the seat of his bicycle to head home, Ben knew that his task was only just beginning. It lay before him like Level 7 in GameCube's Labors of Hercules (ESRB Rating T for Teen). He'd have to get to the other malls and disable their kiosks. He knew that, one way or another, it was up to him.

He was going to have to save America, one mall at a time.

TAKE IT FROM ME, KID

BY David L. Harrison

They used to toss me in the air,
Pat my fanny, muss my hair,
Feed me candy, read me books,
Give me lovey-dovey looks,
Kiss me on the nose.

They used to buy me all the toys
Specially made for little boys—
Wagons, racing cars, trains,
Action figures, model planes—
Now? It's dumb old clothes.

Growing up isn't fair!
You trade toys for underwear!

They used to treat me like a kid,
I miss the old days when they did,
They say that's how it goes.

The teens are going to be the pits—
Shaving, dating, working, zits—
It's all a plot! Whatever you do,
Listen to what I'm telling you!
Don't let them start with clothes!

A PET FOR CALVIN

BY Barbara Robinson

Calvin McCandless thought he might be the only fourth-grade kid in Homer Applegate Elementary School who didn't have a pet. But he wasn't sure about that—some of those kids were girls, and they didn't talk to him about pets or anything else.

His best friend, Roger Stratton, had two pets—a dog and a hamster.

"I *don't* have two pets," Roger always said when this subject came up. "I have a dog. My sister has the hamster. I don't even *like* the hamster."

"But you have two pets in your house," Calvin insisted.

He knew that his friends sometimes got tired of hearing him complain this way, but he couldn't help it.

Probably kids who had pets—dogs, cats, gerbils…a kid in the fifth grade had a ferret—kids who *had* them were so used to having them that they didn't even think about it.

"You don't even think about it," he told Joe Coolidge. "You've got your dog, he's always there…"

"I do too think about it," Joe said. "I *have* to think about it. I have to feed him, and walk him, because in our dumb neighborhood he can't just run free. Tell ya what, Calvin, you can walk my dog if you want to. That would be outside…do you still get wheezy from animals outside?"

Calvin sighed. "In or out," he said, "it doesn't matter." He spoke from experience because his parents did once let him bring a dog home, but before they were even in the house, his eyes had closed up and he couldn't breathe.

"Outstanding!" his grandmother said when she heard about this. "Were they trying to kill you? Death by dog?"

As always, his kooky grandmother made Calvin laugh and feel better…but, as always, she made his father sigh and roll his eyes.

"Mother," Mr. McCandless said, "don't say things like

that. We thought, maybe, with the new medicine, Calvin could tolerate—"

"A short-haired dog," Calvin's mother put in. "It was a short-haired dog."

"Not short enough," his grandmother said...but then she hugged everybody, to show that she wasn't really mad at them, that she was just sad for Calvin.

There was a possibility that Calvin would outgrow his wheeziness, but that would be a long time to wait. Besides, would he still need a pet when he was grown up? His father didn't seem to need one, although maybe he would if it weren't for Calvin's allergy.

"Not at all," his father said. "I have you, and your baby sister, and your mother. I have my job and our home and things to do...like today, I have to go to Home Depot, and I have to watch the ball game, and I have to spade up the vegetable patch. Want to come along?"

Of course he did want to. This was what they did every Saturday: Home Depot, ball game, some house chore.

The Home Depot was always fun, and then the Red Sox won, and now he could dig up dirt and get chore points for it. It was great dirt, too—loose and loamy—and he liked to pick up a shovelful and run it through his fingers.

He made a small cone of the dirt, and with a stick he made a careful hole in the middle, like a model of Mount Vesuvius...and up through the hole came, not hot lava, but a worm.

It stood up—which Calvin had never seen a worm do, but of course this one was in a hole, which helped—and it looked at him.

He was so sure of this that after a second or two he said "Hello"...even though he knew the worm couldn't hear him. He knew, from science class, that worms didn't have ears.

Worms didn't have much of anything, really, except what the science teacher called "sensory receptors"—"Like gooseflesh," the teacher had said, "when you're chilly or scared." Or, Calvin thought, like the funny thrilly feeling in the soles of your feet when you step, barefoot, onto sand and gravel.

Worms, he assumed, must be all feeling, and he reached out to touch this worm. His fingers were inky, from keeping score in the ball game, and he left a black mark on the worm, which wriggled back into the hole.

"Calvin!" his mother called. "It's almost dinnertime. You need to come in and wash up."

To his amazement, the worm wriggled back out and…looked at him again.

He picked it all up—mound of dirt, worm, extra dirt, pieces of grass and leaves and twigs that were lying around—and carried it to where his father had been planting squash seeds, saved from last year in a plastic container.

The plastic container made a perfect worm house, he thought, and added some more grass and twigs and, later, a cover of plastic wrap, with airholes, of course.

Last of all, he wrote SPOT on a piece of tablet paper and taped it to the container. It was the perfect name for his worm, he thought, looking at his own inky finger.

He didn't mention the worm to anyone, but he didn't deliberately *not* mention the worm either. The subject didn't come up, and the only family member who would be interested was his baby sister, and she would just want to eat it.

That night he put the worm house on the shelf above

his bed, with his important things—his baseball cards and signed program, his Morphagon transformer, his Coke bottle that fell from the third floor of the school and didn't break—and before he went to sleep, he took the plastic wrap off and very gently poked around in the dirt till he found the worm, curled up. He stirred the dirt a little more, and the worm curled up a little more, and went back to sleep.

He checked up on his worm, off and on, the next day, but there wasn't much he could do for it. It didn't need water or food…but it did need dirt. Tomorrow, after school, he would take care of his worm's dirt.

At first he thought he would just add dirt, but maybe this was like Kitty Litter that had to be changed, according to his friend John Hazeltine, who had two cats.

"Gotta change the Kitty Litter," John would say, and he would go change the Kitty Litter while Calvin and Roger or Joe would hang around and wait for him to come out and ride bikes.

Of course John could just throw out the old Kitty Litter, but Calvin had to empty the dirt into his mother's big mixing bowl, then transfer his worm into new dirt in the worm house.

He probably likes it in the bowl, Calvin thought, *because there's lots more room. Maybe he thinks it's vacation.*

He scooped up a handful of dirt, and worm, and put it all back in the plastic container on nice new dirt. He could tell—he *thought* he could tell—that his worm liked it because he wriggled right down in, and when Calvin looked in the side of the container, his worm looked back.

On Friday his mother cleaned his room, and she asked him about the container of dirt. "I guess you're growing something in there...seeds...lima beans..."

"No," he said, "it's my worm. He's in there."

"Oh, Calvin!" his mother said. "A worm! You'll just knock that thing down and spill dirt all over your bed."

"Pretty close quarters for a worm," his father said. "It's used to a little more territory."

Calvin suddenly remembered thinking almost that very same thing when he had changed the worm dirt. He had even thought it might seem like a vacation... but a big mixing bowl wasn't much of a vacation when you're used to the whole backyard.

"Of course," his mother said, "I know worms don't have any feelings. . . ."

Wrong, Calvin thought. *They're all feelings, with their*

sensory receptors. A worm could probably feel comfortable...or uncomfortable. Maybe even scared...or nervous... even smart

After supper, he took his mother's garden trowel and scratched out a big path of soft, sifty dirt in the backyard...and, sure enough, Spot wriggled right down into it.

Comfortable, Calvin thought....

In another week or two, he would have changed the dirt six or seven times; he and his worm would have looked at each other through the side of the worm house; he might even have taken him for a very short walk; he would have taken him to school on Bring Your Pet Day...

Now none of those things would happen, and it didn't help to think about them.

The next day was Saturday, and there was Home Depot, but then his parents went to an all-day barbecue, and his grandmother came to stay with him.

"Calvin," she said after lunch, "tell me your life story since last week...all the good stuff."

So he told his grandmother about his worm.

"Outstanding!" she said. "A perfect pet! Your father was right, though. A worm needs a lot of room. We'll get that great big lasagna dish, the glass one... where's the worm?"

"Well, I dumped the dirt, Grandma, so..."

"Hmm. Worm, too, then. Back in the garden?" She didn't wait for him to answer. "Come on, let's see."

Kooky, kooky, he thought as his grandmother fished up a worm, said, "Oh, this is an old one," and dropped it back in the dirt.

"Was your worm very fat?" she asked. "Some worms are."

"I don't know, Grandma...just an average worm."

"Best kind," she said.

Right then Calvin decided to announce that any worm his grandmother produced was his worm. "That's it," he was going to say. "You found my worm!", because it would make her happy, and it wouldn't make any difference to him.

She discarded several worms—"too thin...too lazy"—and then she crowed, "Here we are! If this one could talk, it would say, 'I'm Calvin's worm'...Yes?" And she handed him...Spot.

All Calvin's sensory receptors shivered and tingled. "Yes," he said, his voice a little shaky. "I would know him anywhere," and of course he would, because of the black mark he, Calvin, had put there, on this very worm.

There must be hundreds of worms in this garden. His father had once said, "Too bad I'm not a fisherman, with all these worms." And out of all these worms, his grandmother had found his worm...or, maybe, his worm had found his grandmother, because he had heard her say, "That's some outstanding worm. Stood right up in the dirt."

Now Spot had curled up in the palm of his hand, so Calvin had to use his other hand to scoop dirt into the lasagna dish.

"This is just for now," he told Spot—because maybe his science teacher was right about worms and ears, but even so, it didn't seem right to have a pet and never talk to it. "But next Saturday, at Home Depot, we'll get a really big plastic box to be your house, and a lot of new dirt, and one of those toy ladders that you see in hamster cages..."

By next week, he would have changed the dirt at least twice. "Gotta change the worm dirt!" he would say; he and Spot would have looked at each other each morning and night through the side of the worm house; he would have taken Spot on a walk—just like now, on the palm of his hand.

And this year, on Bring Your Pet Day, he would be the only fourth-grade kid in Homer Applegate Elementary School—maybe the only kid anywhere!—who had a worm for a pet.

THE CHINESE BOY

BY Clyde Robert Bulla

Jon-Tom lived in the country with his father and mother. To him, their farm was the whole world. Then he started school, and he began to learn that the world went on and on, farther and wider than he could ever know.

School was a long way off. To get there, he had to walk across two fields, through the woods, and down a lane. The schoolhouse had only one room. There were small desks and seats down in front for the younger boys and girls. For the older ones, there were bigger seats and desks toward the back of the room.

Jon-Tom was the youngest and the smallest. When the others chose up sides for their games, they hardly ever chose him. On the playground he was almost always alone.

He liked school better when they were inside. He could listen to the teacher and the older boys and girls. That was how he first learned about people in other lands.

In the fourth grade, he still hadn't grown much. He was used to being alone on the playground. And something good had happened to him. Now he had his own geography book. It was the biggest of all his schoolbooks. In it were pictures of people from other lands, with maps that showed where they lived.

He lay awake at night and thought about the world. He wondered what it would be like to have a friend from far away. Sometimes it took him a long time to go to sleep.

One morning he started off for school through a mist that hung in the air like smoke. At first he could see only a little way, but by the time he came to the school lane, the mist was breaking up.

The lane ran along the edge of a pasture. There was a hill in the pasture and a cottonwood tree on the hill. Under the cottonwood he saw something he had never seen there before. Through the mist it looked like a tiny house on wheels. He thought he saw a horse tied to the tree.

At school no one said anything about the house and the horse. He began to wonder if he had really seen them.

Before noon, the mist cleared away, and the autumn day was crisp and fine. The teacher opened the door to let the sun shine in.

Jon-Tom felt restless. He kept wanting to look back at the door.

At last he did look back. A boy was standing in the doorway.

He was just the size of Jon-Tom. He wore a round cap and a jacket and long trousers. His eyes were narrow and dark and bright. He looked like a boy from China that Jon-Tom had seen in his geography book. China was very far away.

The boy stood there and looked over the whole school. Then he came straight to Jon-Tom.

Jon-Tom made room at his desk. The boy sat down. He looked very serious, but he smiled when Jon-Tom smiled.

At noon they went outside together. No one seemed to notice the new boy, and Jon-Tom was glad. He wanted the boy to stay with him and be his friend. They sat on the grass in a corner of the school yard. Jon-

Tom opened his lunch box and set it between them. The new boy was very polite and hardly ate at all.

Jon-Tom asked, "Are you Chinese?"

The boy didn't answer, but it was plain from his face and his clothes that he *was* Chinese.

After lunch, they sat together again, and Jon-Tom showed him his books and drew him pictures.

When school was out, the Chinese boy motioned for Jon-Tom to follow him.

There was a hedge on one side of the school yard, and they slipped through it.

They climbed the hill to the cottonwood tree where the little house was. There *was* a horse tied to the tree. He was yellow and bony and old.

A man and woman came out of the house. They looked as if they might be the boy's father and mother. The boy spoke to them in a strange language. They bowed to Jon-Tom, and he bowed back.

They all sat on the ground and drank tea out of blue cups without handles. They had bowls of rice. They ate the rice with chopsticks—Jon-Tom, too. He was surprised at how easy it was.

By that time the sun was low. Jon-Tom said good-bye.

The boy and the man and woman stood in a row and bowed to him, and he bowed to them.

At home he talked about the Chinese boy. His father and mother listened and said nothing at all.

But in the morning his mother said, "Shall I put another cookie in your lunch for your friend?" She looked at Jon-Tom's father. Jon-Tom knew by the way they smiled at each other that they hadn't believed him.

All at once he felt sad and terribly lonely.

"No," he said. "My friend may not be there."

There was no mist that morning. When he came to the school lane, he looked across the pasture to the hill and the cottonwood tree. The horse and the little house were gone. He knew his friend was gone, too, and would never come back.

A long time afterward, Jon-Tom went to see the schoolhouse. There were only a few bricks and stones to show where it had been.

He stayed for a while on the old playground. He remembered the boys and girls he had known there, and the one he remembered best was the Chinese boy.

HEROES AND VILLAINS

BY Liam Kuhn

Deep beneath the city sewers, in a dark and secret underground lair, Simon Nefarious—supervillain extraordinaire—plotted something dastardly devious and wickedly evil.

"At last," he said to no one in particular, "my plan is nearly complete. By this time tomorrow night, I'll have the entire city in my grasp! Muhahahah!" He twisted his handlebar mustache and cackled a hideous laugh that shook the walls and woke the lizards and bats and snakes he kept as pets.

Meanwhile, in a warm and comfortable suburban home fifteen miles away, Junior McGruder sat alone at the dinner table, watching the hands of the clock tick by. Junior had no appetite. Or rather, he had no appetite for mushy peas and slimy mashed potatoes. He had plenty of appetite for great big bowls of mint-chocolate-chip ice cream like the one his mother was eating in the other room while watching the evening news.

"Finish those vegetables, young man," she called in to Junior.

"What if I drank an extra glass of milk instead?" he asked.

"No."

"What if I promised to eat *twice* as many vegetables tomorrow?"

"No."

"What if I ate spinach for breakfast for a whole month?"

"No."

"What if—"

"No. No. No! No dessert until those peas and potatoes are gone!"

"Why doesn't Dad have to eat *his* dinner?"

Mrs. McGruder walked into the kitchen and began washing her bowl in the sink. "Your father has to eat his dinner, too," she said.

"Oh, yeah? Then where is he?" Junior asked.

Good question. Where *was* Mr. McGruder? For the

third time this week, he was late for dinner. And it was only Wednesday!

Mr. McGruder was an important lawyer who worked long hours in the city and sometimes had to take the late train home, but this was ridiculous. It was nearly Junior's bedtime! Plus, he'd promised to help Junior with his Science Fair project.

Junior was just about to complain to his mom when the voice on the television became louder.

"We interrupt that delightful story about baby pandas at the zoo to bring you this breaking news," the newscaster said. "Minutes ago, four masked men attempting a robbery at the downtown First City Bank were apprehended and placed in police custody. Eyewitnesses say the men were about to escape with over five million dollars in stolen cash when Wonderman, the caped superhero, once again came to the rescue."

Junior and his mother ran into the living room. There on TV, they saw four scruffy men in handcuffs being pushed into police cars and driven off to jail. In the background, shaking hands with the chief of police, was Wonderman. He wore a yellow utility belt over bright red tights and a long blue cape. He smiled at the chief and flew off into the night.

Mrs. McGruder looked relieved. "Junior," she said. "Do you know how Wonderman got so big and strong?"

"Let me guess," said Junior.

"By listening to his mother and eating his vegetables," she said.

"Whatever," Junior mumbled under his breath. But he went back into the kitchen, held his nose, and shoveled the cold, lumpy food into his mouth.

Upstairs in his room, Junior lay on his bed surrounded by books about circuitry and electronics. The Science Fair was two days away. All the other kids were building baking-soda volcanoes or solar systems out of Styrofoam balls, but Junior wanted to do something better, something nobody had ever done before. He wanted to build a real, working robot. The only problem? Junior didn't know the first thing about robots. But his dad did. His dad knew everything. And he'd promised to help. So where was he?

Junior opened one of the books and tried to make

sense out of it, but it was very confusing and a little boring, and after a while, he fell asleep.

When he woke up a few hours later, Junior heard voices talking softly in the kitchen. He got out of bed and sneaked downstairs to poke his head into the kitchen. There was his father, still dressed in his suit and tie. He was sitting across the table from Junior's mother, looking very tired while reluctantly finishing his plate of cold peas and potatoes.

Whatever they were talking about was very important. Junior could tell because they were whispering the way adults whisper when they have important things to say: way too loud.

"I don't know, honey," his father said. "I'm just tired of the whole thing."

"What do you mean? You did a great job today," his mother said.

"But the hours are killing me. And I hate being away from home so much."

"I know, but it's part of the job," she said.

"I miss spending time with you and Junior. He was already asleep when I went up to say hello," he said.

"Junior had a long day. We got into a debate about

vegetables—I'm for them, he's against!" They both laughed, but Junior didn't see what was so funny. Those peas were gross! "And then he tired himself out working on his science project."

"Oh! I forgot all about it! I said I'd help him tonight, and now it's too late."

"You were busy. He'll understand," she said.

But Mr. McGruder shook his head. "I don't know," he said. "I remember how mad I got at my dad whenever he broke a promise."

"This is different, though. They need you in the city. Nobody else can do what you do. Someday, Junior will understand."

"I don't care if they need me in the city. My son needs me here!" Mr. McGruder said.

"What if you took a vacation? Or cut back on your hours?" she said.

"It's not the kind of job you can take a vacation from."

"It's not the kind of job you can quit, either," she said.

"We'll see about that."

* * *

Junior had heard enough. His father was thinking about quitting his job? Sure, it'd be nice to spend more time with his dad, but wasn't it Mr. McGruder himself who'd taught Junior that quitting was never the solution to anything?

Junior tiptoed back to his room and turned out the light. He lay in the dark, but couldn't sleep. He was worried about his father. Why was he never home? Why did he look so tired and sound so sad? And why was he talking about quitting?

Junior had no answers. Only more questions. He heard the crickets outside his window and the sound of a night train headed to the city. He heard a lonely dog howl in the dark. Finally, his eyelids grew heavy, and Junior drifted off to sleep.

Junior was dreaming about hitting a walk-off home run to win the World Series when he felt a tickling on his toes. He awoke and saw his father smiling down at him.

"Wake up, sleepyhead," Mr. McGruder said.

"Dad! What are you doing here? Shouldn't you be at work?"

"I'm taking the day off. I'm surprising your mom

with breakfast in bed, and then I'll drive you to school."

When they got to the kitchen, it was already a mess. Sure, Mr. McGruder might be a smart guy and a hotshot lawyer, but he was definitely NOT a cook. Broken eggshells were everywhere and French toast was dripping from the ceiling. Pancake batter slopped down the sides of the cabinets, and Chuckles-the-Dog licked a puddle of orange juice off the floor.

As they were cleaning up, Mrs. McGruder walked in. "Oh, my goodness!" she said. "It looks like a bomb went off in here!" The McGruder men looked at her, looked at the mess, and broke out laughing.

"Mom, this was supposed to be a surprise!" Junior said.

"It certainly is," she said.

"Sorry about the mess," said Mr. McGruder. "Hope you like your eggs scrambled. And your toast, and your pancakes, and everything else!"

"Thank you," she said. "This was so sweet of you. But maybe next time, just pick up bagels!"

"Gimme a break, I'm not a superhero!" Mr. McGruder said, and Mrs. McGruder laughed so hard she nearly shot orange juice through her nose.

After breakfast, Mr. McGruder drove Junior to school.

"Remember," he said, "we'll get to work on that robot as soon as you come home, okay?"

"I can't wait, Dad," Junior said, and he smiled bigger than he ever had before.

Meanwhile, a train carrying two tons of smuggled explosives headed north toward the city.

Everything was proceeding exactly according to Simon Nefarious's terrible plan. His legion of small-time crooks and evil henchmen was in position to receive the explosives and bury them in strategic locations throughout the city. Once everything was in place, Nefarious would contact the mayor and demand control of the city. Twisting his silly mustache and cackling his awful laugh, Nefarious said to himself, "If the mayor won't obey my orders, I'll detonate the explosives and reduce the entire city to smoldering rubble! Muhahahah!"

At school, Junior got an A-plus on his vocabulary quiz, hit a home run in kickball, and watched a filmstrip about his favorite dinosaur, the triceratops. Even though it was such a good day, he couldn't wait for it to end. The moment the final bell rang, he ran all the way home, excited to start working on the robot with his dad.

When he got home, Junior ran through the living room, through the kitchen, up the stairs, into his room, into his parents' room, back down the stairs, through the kitchen again, and into the basement. But his father was nowhere to be found. Junior ran out into the backyard and nearly knocked over his mother.

"Mom, quick, where's Dad?" he asked.

"I'm sorry, Junior," she said. "Your father had to go into the city this afternoon."

"But he took the day off."

"I know. He'll be back as soon as he can."

"But he promised!" Junior said.

"I'm sorry," was all Mrs. McGruder could say.

Junior stomped back into the house and sulked his way up to his room. He slammed the door shut and tried to work on the robot himself. It was no use. He was so mad, he couldn't concentrate. What was going on with his dad? Why was he running off to the city all the time? Why did he make promises he never kept? Junior needed to get to the bottom of this. "I'm going to sneak into the city and find my father," he said to himself.

Sneaking out of the house was easy; Junior quietly crept out the door while his mother wasn't looking.

Finding the train station was easy; they passed it every day on the way to school. Getting on the right train was easy; the train conductor was friendly and helpful, even though he did find it a bit suspicious that Junior was traveling alone.

But once the train arrived in the city, nothing was easy, and Junior panicked. He'd been to the city many times before, but never without his mom or dad or a teacher on a field trip. The buildings seemed bigger, the traffic louder, the people ruder and in more of a rush. How could his dad do this every single day?

Junior got pushed around in a crowd of people and had no idea where to turn. He was scared and angry and realized it was a mistake to sneak out of the house and into the city, no matter how upset he was with his father. Just as he was about to give up and turn around and go home, he looked across the street and saw an enormous, gleaming office building taller than anything he'd ever seen. *That must be where my dad works,* Junior thought. People wearing suits like the one his dad wore and carrying briefcases like the one his dad carried walked in and out of the office building. One person even looked like his dad. In fact, it *was* Junior's dad!

But where was he going? Mr. McGruder was quickly walking away from the building toward an old warehouse with boarded-up windows and rotting wooden doors. Just as Junior was about to call out to him, Mr. McGruder ducked inside the abandoned warehouse. Junior waited for the streetlight to change, looked both ways, and followed after his father.

It took Junior's eyes a few seconds to adjust to the darkness once he was inside. When he looked around, he saw big wooden crates and rusty oil drums. Bats swooped down from the rafters, and furry gray rats skittered along the walls. But no sign of his father! Junior was terribly frightened now and regretted coming to the city. He was about to cry out "Dad!" when he heard a loud crashing sound.

Junior hid behind a row of oil drums and looked to his left. There, in the center of the warehouse, on a huge box labeled EXPLOSIVES, sat Simon Nefarious, the world's vilest man (and also owner of the world's silliest mustache and worst cackle). Nefarious was stomping up and down on the box of explosives, holding a detonator in one hand and a cell phone in the other.

"If you think I'm bluffing, you're making a huge mistake, Mr. Mayor!" he screamed into the cell phone. "I'll give you five seconds to change your mind, or else I'll blow the whole place up!"

Junior couldn't believe what he was hearing!

"Five...four..." Nefarious began his evil countdown.

Junior had to do something.

"Three..."

But what could he do?

"Two..."

He was only a kid!

"One!"

As Nefarious was about to press the button and detonate the explosives, a voice called out from above: "Stop right there, Nefarious!" Junior looked up and saw...Wonderman!

Wonderman swooped down from the balcony on a steel cable, with his bright blue cape swooshing behind, and landed on the crate of explosives. He knocked the detonator from Nefarious's hand and the two began to fight.

This is incredible, Junior thought. But where was his father?

There was no time to think about that, though, because all of a sudden Nefarious grabbed Wonderman around the neck and put him in a painful headlock. He knocked Wonderman to the ground and reached for the detonator. Junior had to think, and fast.

Suddenly he remembered the chapter on circuitry and electronics he'd read the night before. If he could find a way to disrupt the electrical current leading to the lights, he might be able to help Wonderman. He scampered along the wall and found the fuse box. He climbed on an oil drum, opened the box, and saw a maze of wires, switches, and knobs. Which one controlled the lights? He tried to remember what he had read. He looked over his shoulder and saw Nefarious inching closer to the detonator. He had no time to think, he had to do something!

Junior pulled wires and flipped switches. The warehouse went completely dark. He heard Nefarious curse, and then the sounds of the superhero and villain battling in the dark. He heard punches thrown and bodies slammed into the ground. Finally, he heard Wonderman say, "I've got you now, Nefarious," and he heard the click of Wonderman's indestructible supersteel handcuffs as they snapped on Simon's wrists. Junior turned the lights back on.

He expected to see Wonderman standing triumphantly over the bad guy in the trademark superhero pose: hands on hips, chest puffed out, cape billowing majestically in the breeze. But when he looked at Wonderman, he saw…his dad!

Mr. McGruder was dressed in Wonderman's tights. He had Wonderman's utility belt wrapped around his waist and Wonderman's cape flapping behind his back. On the ground, torn off during the fight, was the mask that concealed Wonderman's secret identity. Could it be? Junior's dad *was* Wonderman! When Junior realized this, he nearly fainted. Instead, he stayed hidden to find out what would happen next.

"I heard you were quitting, Wonderman," Nefarious groaned. "I thought you'd given up on the whole superhero thing."

"Not yet, Nefarious," Mr. McGruder said, and he quickly pulled his mask back on before Nefarious looked up at him. "I can't quit, not with scum like you around. Aren't you ever going to give up?"

"Never!" Nefarious cackled, but it was the cackle of a broken, defeated man.

"You don't get tired of this?"

"Never," Nefarious said again, but with even less enthusiasm.

"Well, *I* get tired of it. Real tired," Wonderman said.

"Today was supposed to be my day off. I was supposed to spend time with my son. Now it's too late. I'm sick and tired of you bad guys always ruining everything!" Wonderman shoved Nefarious and then slumped down next to him on the box of explosives.

"Hey, settle down," Nefarious said. "You won. It's over."

"Don't you see? It's not over. It's never over. All I wanted was a nice quiet day at home with my family. All I wanted was to help my boy build a robot for his Science Fair. Was that too much to ask? I didn't ask to save the world. I didn't want to be a hero." Wonderman began to cry. "I just wanted to be a good dad."

Even the evilest supervillain from the deepest, darkest sewer has a heart, and when Nefarious saw Wonderman in tears, he began to cry, too. "I didn't know," he said. "I'm sorry."

"Forget it," Wonderman said. "You're a Bad Guy; you were just doing your job. But now I've got to sit here and wait for the police to arrive; I need to file a report, fill out all that paperwork…I just wish I were home with my son. I made a promise, and I meant to keep it."

"I know what you mean," Nefarious said.

"You do?"

"Of course. I've got kids of my own. Two wonderful girls. I missed their soccer match last night because I was in my secret underground lair, plotting to take over the city. It was the play-offs, too."

"That's awful."

"I know! It went down to penalty kicks, and they won! I was the only parent not there."

The superhero and supervillain sadly shook their heads.

Junior had seen enough surprises for one day and decided the best thing for him to do would be to head back home before his mom knew he was gone.

Nefarious turned to Wonderman and said, "You should go. Get back to your wife and son. If you leave now, you'll still have time to help him with his science project."

"Nice try, Nefarious. You just want me to leave before the cops get here so you can get away."

"Don't worry about me. Those days are over. I'm done as a supervillain. I'm retiring. I'm going to get rid of all these explosives, apologize to the mayor and the people of this city, pay my debt to society, and try to be a better father."

"How do I know you're not lying?" Wonderman

asked. "How do I know you won't be back here tomorrow, trying to take over the world again?"

"What's the point of taking over the world if you can't watch your girls play soccer?"

"You're right."

"I need to spend some time where I'm not the bad guy, for a change."

"Good luck," the superhero said.

"Thanks. You, too," the supervillain said. And the men went their not-so-separate ways.

Junior came home and tiptoed up the stairs to his room. He had no idea when his father—the superhero!—would get home, so he began working on the robot by himself. His mother knocked on the door and came in with a plate of cookies and a glass of milk.

"You're awfully quiet in here. Everything all right?" she asked.

"It sure is," Junior said.

"I hope you're not too upset with Dad for having to work today. I know you were looking forward to spending some time with him."

"I was. But it's okay. Whatever he had to do, I'm sure it was important."

"You're important, too. We want you to know that," she said.

"I know," Junior said. "Hey, Mom?"

"Yes?"

"Know anything about robots?"

Junior McGruder and his mother worked late into the night building the robot. When Mr. McGruder came home, he looked exhausted but happier than they'd seen him in weeks. The McGruders ate dinner together as a family, then put the finishing touches on Junior's Science Fair project. Junior decided not to tell his mom about what he'd witnessed or the discovery he'd made. In fact, he wasn't going to tell his dad, either. He wasn't going to tell anyone. Some secrets are too good to share.

After school the next day, Junior came tearing through the door with a big smile on his face.

"How'd you do, honey?" his mom asked.

"Did you win?" his dad asked.

"No," Junior said. "I came in third. But all the kids loved the robot, and I had a lot of fun working on it. And it was way cooler than a baking-soda volcano."

Junior gave his parents a big hug.

"What's that for?" his dad asked.

"Everything," Junior said.

Later that night, the McGruders went to the ice-cream parlor to celebrate. Mrs. McGruder was happy her family was all together again; Mr. McGruder was happy just being a dad; and Junior was happy because what he'd known all along—that his father was a hero—had turned out to be the truth.

They finished their milk shakes and got ready to leave. Suddenly they heard a loud, hideous cackle that could belong only to one man—Simon Nefarious. But when they turned around, the only thing they saw was a happy man twisting his silly mustache, sharing a banana split with his family.

THE MAROONED BOY

Retold by Richard Alan Young
from a Caddo Indian Story

Along rivers that ran southward in Texas, Oklahoma, Arkansas, and Louisiana, there once lived a powerful nation of Indians we call the Caddo. Each Caddo village had over a dozen houses, separated by gardens, standing along a crooked river like beads on a string. Each house was made of mud plaster with a high roof of prairie grass. Each house had a low doorway facing the river.

In each tall house lived a large family with a father and mother, children, grandparents, and sometimes aunts, uncles, or cousins, too. The men and boys hunted on the nearby prairies and in the narrow stands of trees along the rivers. The women and girls worked around the house and tended the gardens. They filled gourd bowls at the river for watering the gardens of tobacco, pumpkins, gourds, corn, beans, and squash. The Caddo loved a vegetable stew called "the Three Sisters," made from corn, beans, and squash cooked together.

Sometimes boys fished in the river, even going out in canoes in the heat of the day, but they never waded or swam in the river because of a monster that lived underwater. Every day, just at sunset, the great and terrible Water Panther came up from the river bottom to eat! He ate careless animals or foolish children who came too close...or stayed too long...beside the river as the sun went down.

The Water Panther was longer than two canoes. His head was almost as big as a house. His yellow catlike eyes were bigger around than the largest pumpkin. His mouth was as big as a doorway, and filled with many teeth sharper than knives of flint. The Water Panther was covered with sleek, shiny black fur. He had thick horns like those of a buffalo, but much larger and longer, for he was bigger than any buffalo that ever lived.

When the Water Panther came up from the river bottom to hunt at sundown, the Caddo could see him from the safety of their doorways. The tips of his horns showed above the surface of the water as he swam back and forth. But the Water Panther never came out of the river and was seldom seen except at sunset. So, when the sun was going down, all the Caddo people stayed in their houses and ate their supper. After darkness fell, the Water Panther went to the river bottom to sleep.

One evening the Caddo people sat cross-legged around the fire in their houses, eating their Three Sisters out of gourd bowls. Outside, in the yellow light of sunset, they heard a sound that struck fear into their hearts—the sound of a paddle slapping the water as someone came downriver in a canoe.

Who would be so foolish as to travel on the river just at sunset, when the great Water Panther was hunting? Far upstream, on the prairies, the river was so narrow and shallow that there was no room for a huge monster to live. Only someone from far upstream would make the terrible mistake of being on the river at this hour!

The Caddo boys ran to their doorways. They saw a canoe. A man sat in the back, paddling. A woman sat in the front. In the middle of the canoe was a large pile of brown rolls of something furry.

Behind the canoe, the Water Panther's horns were following! The horns rose higher and higher out of the river, but the people in the canoe could not see them. Soon the top of the Water Panther's head came out of the water…then his eyes…then his huge mouth.

He ate the man in one bite, then swam up and ate the woman in one bite!

The Water Panther sank beneath the dark waters and dove to the river bottom to sleep.

The canoe floated to the shore by the village.

The Caddo people ran from their houses to the river-bank, and the older boys pulled the canoe up on the grass. Everyone gathered around and looked at what was in the canoe. The brown furry things were buffalo-hide robes, rolled up in a pile for trade. The Peace Chief, who led the village in times of good hunting and good harvest, came forward and spoke.

"These poor people came downstream from the tall-grass prairies where there is no Water Panther in the narrow creeks. They brought robes of buffalo hide to trade with us. But the Water Panther ate these poor people! Now we cannot make trade with them."

One young man said, "Let us, each family, take one robe. The dead will not miss them."

"That would not be right," answered the Peace Chief, "for we would be giving nothing in return."

Just then, one of the rolled-up buffalo robes moved a little!

An old woman, whose only child had long ago married and moved to another village, guessed what was moving in the robe. She lifted the buffalo robe and opened it.

Inside was a baby boy, just waking up from his nap. The Water Panther had not seen the baby wrapped in the robe, and had not smelled the baby, because the smell of buffalo was strong in the canoe.

"I will take this boy," said the old woman, "and raise him as my grandson. I will teach him to be brave, strong, and truthful. In repayment for this kindness, let us, each family, take one buffalo robe from the baby's canoe."

"That is well," said the Peace Chief, "and you are kind."

Each father stepped up and took a robe for his family. The families returned to their houses. The old woman rocked the baby in her arms. She would no longer have to live alone.

Eleven happy summers came and went.

The boy grew up tall, strong, and handsome. The old woman named him Buffalo Robe Boy and taught him well. She had lived a long time, and had learned all of the women's ways, and most of the men's ways as well. She taught him everything she knew that a man would teach a boy. But there was one problem for which she could not give a man's advice.

The Caddo people loved to tease. Buffalo Robe Boy had no living family but the old woman, and they were poor. This meant that almost anyone could tease him, but often he was not permitted to tease back. The old woman teased him gently only when he made a mistake, to help him learn. He knew she teased him because she loved him.

But sometimes the other boys were cruel.

"Grandmother," he asked, "what can I do when I am teased by older boys whose bows and arrows are better than mine?"

The old woman sighed. "Teasing is a part of life. Someday you may pour water on the bean stalk, to water it, and miss, and the water may go on the squash, which I have already watered. If that happens, I may tease and say, 'You will drown Squash Sister, while Bean Sister starves!' You should laugh and say, 'It is true. I should be more careful.'

"An older boy may say to you, 'Your bow dresses poorly, for my bow wears pretty beadwork!' You should laugh and say, 'It is true. My bow dresses poorly. But the beadwork hides your bow's eyes, for it cannot see to shoot as straight as mine!'"

Buffalo Robe Boy laughed.

"But," said the old woman, "if an older boy says to you, 'You do not have a good heart,' you should frown and say, 'That is not true. You should always tell the truth, even when you tease.' Grandson, you should always tell the truth."

The time came that winter for the old woman to die, and go to walk the Star Path with the Ancestors. Buffalo Robe Boy was alone. He had always hunted alone; now he tended the garden alone. He had no living relative; the other boys ignored him. It was worse than the teasing.

And something even more tragic happened that winter. No snow fell, no rain came in early spring. It was a year of drought. The water level in the river fell lower and lower, leaving wide, muddy banks. The water had once been clear and sweet; during the drought, it was stagnant and dirty. The deer and other animals went away downstream in search of better water to drink. The village was in peril!

The Water Panther got angry! With the animals gone, he wanted people to eat! With the water in the river so low, the Caddo boys could see his horns almost every hour of the day and night. He swam up and down the riverbed, hoping to catch a boy or girl coming down for water. The people knew that the Water Panther took a nap in the hottest part of the day, for at that hour, his horns were not seen. But even then the people were afraid to get dirty water at the muddy riverbank. Their gardens were dying. With no animals to hunt, and no gardens to harvest, the people were starving.

Because the village was in great danger, the War Chief took charge. He called a council of all the fathers of the village.

"We will all die, and our families will die, if we do not do hard things," said the War Chief. "If you have a pet, cook it and eat it. And that boy that was not born a Caddo, we must not let him eat among us any longer.

"This is my plan…"

The men listened sadly.

The next day, when the sun was high and hot, the monster was asleep in the river bottom. All the people of the village got in canoes and paddled to an island in a wide part of the river. On the island were trees and in the trees were birds' nests. The older boys climbed the trees and brought down the eggs from the nests. The people built fires, and cooked eggs and wild onions on hot rocks. It was the best meal they had eaten in many days.

Then the War Chief made a big show of yawning and pretending to be sleepy.

"Let us all take a nap," he said. "The Water Panther will be asleep a while longer."

When everyone was lying on the warm sand, asleep or pretending to be asleep, the War Chief crept down the line, silently touching and waking everyone.

Everyone except the boy who was not born a Caddo.

As quietly as hunters stalking deer, the people sadly and silently paddled away from the island and back upstream to the village.

Buffalo Robe Boy awoke from his nap to see that the

people were gone. The sun was setting, and he was alone, marooned on the island. He was not angry...only sad.

As the boy stood looking toward the village, upriver in the distance, the Water Panther's horns broke the dirty surface of the river. The monster lifted its huge head out of the muddy water. The Water Panther's giant yellow cat's eyes blinked and the creature spoke in a voice that rumbled like distant thunder.

"Boy...why are you here?"

The boy stepped back a step or two. He tasted bitter fear in his mouth. But he answered bravely. "The people of the village marooned me here" is all he said.

The creature thought to himself: *If I eat this boy in a single bite, I will have one good supper. If I trick the people of the village into thinking I am their friend, I will eat many good suppers.*

Then the Water Panther said aloud, "Boy...do you climb upon my neck! Do you hold fast to my horns! I will swim and carry you across to the village."

The boy stood silently for a moment. He, too, was thinking to himself. *I have always been told that the Water Panther is the enemy of the people,* he thought. But he had the choice of starving to death on the island or risking being eaten by the Water Panther.

He chose to ride the beast.

Buffalo Robe Boy walked into the muddy water, up to his knees. He climbed up to ride on the creature's neck. He grabbed the ends of the two long, thick horns and held on. The great Water Panther turned and held his huge head above the water as he swam upstream toward the village.

"But you must tell me, Boy..." rumbled the Water Panther, "if you see the Evening Star appear."

"I will tell you," answered the boy. He turned and looked to the west. In the fading light of day, the Evening Star began to faintly shine. "I see the Evening Star," he said.

The Water Panther whipped around and swam quickly back to the island. As the beast sank into the dark river, the boy jumped off just in time.

The next day, the boy sat on the riverbank, staring upstream toward the distant village. He could not swim to the village. He could not swim at all. No Caddo boys living on that river went swimming...the Water Panther might have eaten them!

As the sun sank low in the sky, the horns appeared in the water. The boy stood as the monster reared his ugly head and said: "Do you climb upon my neck! Do you hold fast to my horns! I will swim and carry you across to the village." The boy climbed on the giant neck and gripped the heavy horns again. "But you must tell me, Boy, if you see the Evening Star appear!"

"I…will…tell you," promised the boy. But he did not want to do it.

The monster was halfway to the village when the Evening Star began to glow in the gathering darkness.

"I…see…the Evening Star," said the boy fearfully.

Again the monster twisted quickly around and swam back to the island. The boy jumped off, and the great beast sank beneath the muddy water.

The third day, the boy was so hungry he hunkered down on his heels by the river. He held his arms folded across his stomach and rocked forward and back. As the beast returned at sunset, the boy was so weak he could hardly stand. The monster blinked at the boy and shook water off his long whiskers.

"Do you climb upon my neck! Do you hold fast to my horns! I will swim and carry you across to the village."

The boy slowly climbed on and grabbed the horns. "But you must tell me, Boy, if you see the Evening Star appear."

The boy closed his eyes, and bowed his head, and answered, "If I see it…I will tell you."

The Water Panther swam so close to the village that the boy could hear the distant laughter of the boys and girls in their houses. But then a strange thing happened. In addition to his stomach hurting, his heart began to hurt. He had been taught to always tell the truth. In his silence to the monster, he was not telling the truth.

Buffalo Robe Boy opened his eyes and looked to the west. He saw the Evening Star. But the Evening Star was not walking down the night sky. It was falling slowly toward the earth. It grew larger and larger as it came closer and closer.

The boy could see that the Evening Star was an Indian man, dressed in white deerskin clothing, with long fringe on the sleeves of his shirt. In one hand he carried a bow. In the other he carried a bundle of arrows. He raised the bundle of arrows to his mouth and gripped it with his teeth. He pulled one arrow out of the bundle. He notched the arrow to his bowstring and pointed it down…straight…toward…the boy.

The Evening Star is going to shoot me with his arrow, thought the boy, *to punish me for not telling the truth!*

The Evening Star let the arrow fly. But it did not hit Buffalo Robe Boy.

It was not aimed at him.

The arrow struck the monster between his ribs, piercing his evil heart.

The Water Panther let out a fierce roar and rolled over in the water. The boy jumped off into deep mud and struggled out onto the grass. He turned to see the monster sink below the waves. A dark maroon-colored pool of Water Panther blood spread across the brown river.

The Evening Star floated to the earth like a white catalpa blossom dropping from high in a tree. When his moccasins hit the ground, he became heavy like any Indian man. He walked to Buffalo Robe Boy and laid his hand on the boy's shoulder.

He smiled and said, "Boy, for many years I have tried to kill the great Water Panther and save the Caddo people from this danger. Always before, he saw me coming. But tonight, with you riding on his neck, he was not looking west. Let us go into the village and tell the people how you have helped to save them."

"I am an orphan," said the boy. "I do not need to return to the village. I have made up my mind to go elsewhere."

"Then come with me," said Evening Star, "and we shall walk in the night sky forever. We shall hunt the great animals in the star-pictures." Pointing at the constellations, he called their names: "The Great Bear... the Deer... the Long Snake! And you"—he looked back at the orphan boy—"shall be my arrow carrier."

Evening Star handed the arrow bundle to the boy and took the boy's other hand in his.

Evening Star stepped up—and even though there was nothing there to step on, he rose higher and higher, step after step. The boy rose with him until they were high in the night sky. He let go of the orphan boy's hand, and they walked side by side among the other stars.

"Orphan Star," said Evening Star with a smile, "give me an arrow."

Grinning back, Orphan Star pulled an arrow from the bundle and handed it to his new hunting partner.

Evening Star told the arrow the story of the marooned boy and the great Water Panther. Then he shot the arrow down to the village, where it stuck in the dirt by the council fire. The arrow called all the people together, and they sat cross-legged and listened. The arrow told them the story of Evening Star and his arrow carrier, Orphan Star.

The Caddo people of Oklahoma have told this story over and over for hundreds of years.

And now you may tell it, too.

CLASS TRIP

BY Joseph Robinette

I t was already mid-April. Only six more weeks and school would be over. Wadleigh Harvey Richardson III (most everybody called him Waddy) was one of several students at Wonder Elementary who hated to see school end. It meant work—*hard* work—for three months on the farm. But this year, for the first time since he had been in school, Waddy had something to look forward to between mid-April and summer. A class trip to Baltimore.

Waddy had never been to Baltimore, even though it was only about a hundred miles away. In fact, a lot of the kids in Waddy's class had never been to Baltimore. Several hadn't even been to Washington, D.C., which was only seventy miles away. But Waddy had. The preacher at his church had organized a day trip for his

Sunday-school class two years ago when Waddy was nine. They had seen the Capitol and ridden the elevator to the top of the Washington Monument and gone into the theater where Abraham Lincoln got shot and a few other places that Waddy had forgotten about.

But the trip to Baltimore was going to be more than a day trip. They were going to spend the night in a real nice hotel. One of the teachers had said it was close to the water and also near Camden Yard, where the Baltimore Orioles played baseball. The Orioles were Waddy's favorite team in all the world. Billy Mack Watkins had looked on his baseball schedule and said that the Orioles would be playing in Baltimore the very night they'd be there. They wouldn't be going to the game, of course, but just to be in the same town where the Orioles were playing was good enough for Waddy.

Billy Mack said the game would probably be on the TV at the hotel. Now that wouldn't be such a big deal for most people, since almost everybody got the Orioles' games back home on their TVs. Except for Waddy. The cable line hadn't been strung out as far as the farm yet, and anyway, his father said he probably wouldn't take it even if it became available. "I don't see the need of it," he'd said. The family did have an old

black-and-white set that got just two channels on rab-
bit ears that were covered with tinfoil to help with the
reception.

Waddy and his family were poor, but only in the
sense that they didn't have much money. Their small
farm supplied adequate food. The farmhouse supplied
adequate shelter. And Waddy's parents supplied more
than adequate protection and love. There's not a lot
else a person really needs. But that doesn't mean there
aren't a lot of things a person might *want*—like a motor
scooter or a brand-new hunting gun or video games or
something to *play* the video games on. Waddy wanted
those things and more. But his father had his own ideas
about "wanting things." "A good name is better than
great riches," he would say. What his father meant
was that when people *heard* your name, they thought
highly of you—that you were a good person—reliable
and trustworthy.

In Baltimore, the class was going to see four
things—the aquarium, the B&O Railroad Museum,
Harborplace, and an art museum. Waddy and his
friends were looking forward to everything except the
art museum. But Mrs. Weintraub, their teacher, had
said it would help "round them out."

The school bus got to Baltimore about noon, and the class had a picnic lunch at the aquarium near the rain forest. Then they spent the rest of the afternoon at Harborplace. It was all pretty neat, but it would have been better for Waddy if he'd had more money to spend. On the way to supper, the bus passed right by Camden Yard. It was still about two hours before game time, but the stadium lights were on, and people were already starting to gather. Waddy's heart was practically in his throat. He couldn't believe he'd actually been that close to where the Orioles play, and would be playing that very night!

The hotel was right in the middle of downtown Baltimore, and it was very swanky. Most schools that take class trips—if they're lucky enough to stay overnight—would go to places like Days Inn and Howard Johnson's, which are nice, of course, but not swanky. It seems that a man who used to live in Wonder moved to Baltimore and got rich and bought part of a swanky hotel and made arrangements for the fifth grade to stay there every year. Waddy's father said the man was the only person from Wonder to ever "make good."

There was a problem at the hotel when they got

there. The students were supposed to sleep four to a room, all on the sixth floor. But for some reason, there were *five* boys assigned to Waddy's room. And there couldn't be five in a room, because the fire marshal had said it wouldn't be safe. "We're completely full on the sixth floor," the hotel manager said to Mr. Bernard, the elementary-school principal. "All we have left in the entire hotel is an end room, a single, on the eighth floor."

"Sure hate to put one of the boys up there all by himself," Waddy heard Mr. Bernard say.

"He'll be fine," replied the manager. "We have twenty-four-hour security. Nobody can enter or leave except through the lobby or the fire escape, of course. And only one window opens, for ventilation, and no more than ten inches."

Mr. Bernard thought it over and began to nod as though it seemed okay. Waddy would *not* volunteer to go to that room if Mr. Bernard asked for a volunteer. Any of the other boys would probably love to have a room all by himself. A room where he wouldn't have to share a bed and would have the TV to himself, and he could probably see all of Baltimore and maybe even a little bit of Washington, D.C., from the window up there. Who wouldn't want that room? Waddy. He was probably the only fifth grader, boy or girl, who had never been to a sleepover. He'd been invited, but when he would ask his mother, she would tell him to ask his father, and his father would say, "I don't see the need of it." And that would be that.

Waddy had looked forward to his first trip overnight, staying in a room with three other guys. He knew they wouldn't sleep much, but that was part of the fun of it. *And* Terrell Lathrope had secretly put a deck of cards into his suitcase, and they were going to play penny-ante poker all night long! Waddy didn't know much about playing poker, but he'd saved up fifty-three pennies for the occasion.

The principal turned slowly to the five boys, four of whom wanted the room all to himself. But Mr. Bernard didn't take long to make his decision. The principal went to the same small church that Waddy's family did, and he knew them to be honest and reliable people. Since he didn't know the other boys quite as well, he chose Waddy for the room on the eighth floor. There was a mild protest from the others that made Waddy *pray* Mr. Bernard would change his mind, but it wasn't to be.

Mrs. Clemmenton, another teacher on the trip, escorted Waddy up to his room. "You should be very proud of yourself, Wadleigh," she said. "Mr. Bernard picked you for the single room because you are trustworthy." But he wished one of the other boys had been considered trustworthier. "Yes, ma'am," he said to Mrs. Clemmenton.

When they reached the room, Mrs. C went over Mr. Bernard's instructions. Waddy wasn't allowed to leave the room except for "fire or other act of God." He wasn't to open the door for anybody. No opening of the window either. Under intense questioning, the manager had admitted that a boy of Waddy's size might be able to squeeze through the window "if he wanted to." Mrs. C said good night to Waddy and told him to be careful.

He couldn't leave his room. He couldn't open the door. He couldn't even crack the window. How much more careful could he be?

"Trustworthy," Waddy muttered, half aloud, as he began to unpack. "Some reward."

From his suitcase, he withdrew a pair of freshly washed corduroy pants. ("No blue jeans in a city like Baltimore," his mother had said.) A nicely pressed shirt.

Socks, underwear, and pajamas. ("The ones without holes.") Toothbrush and toothpaste. ("Remember, brush at least three minutes up and down, not just across.") And soap. ("In case the hotel should run out.") It was a nice enough room. And it had plenty of soap. *But* no buddies, no sleepover, and *no* poker.

Well, at least he had a bed all to himself. He pulled the bedcovers down and fluffed up the pillows. Without even lying down, he knew this bed would be more comfortable than the cot he slept on at home. That was something, anyway.

The room was a little too warm, even though it was getting a bit chilly outside. Waddy decided to do the only thing he knew to do, even though he'd promised not to. He would crack open the window. He pushed back the drapes and was suddenly awestruck by what he saw. Downtown Baltimore, spangled in a million lights or more, stretched out in front of him. He was so taken by the scene that it took him a full thirty seconds to discover the most awesome part of the nighttime spectacle—Camden Yard in all its glory, no more than a couple of blocks away.

Part of the stadium wall, which was nearest Wadleigh, partially obscured the outfield. But beyond that, he could actually see the pitcher, catcher, batter, and infielders. It was hard to make out which team was which, or whether the ball was actually hit or missed. But he could see the players moving about and the teams changing sides at the end of an inning. Wadleigh Harvey Richardson III was actually watching a Baltimore Orioles baseball game, live and in person, even though it *was* at some distance.

There they were: Michaels, Wilson, Hernandez, Johnson, and the others, and, of course, Waddy's favorite—Cig Cartwright—all looking like miniature players on a board game. It was possible that Waddy couldn't actually see Cig, who was the second-string catcher and might be in the dugout. He had always been a dangerous power hitter and could swat the ball a long distance *if* he connected with it. But that was a big if. Cig struck out more often than he hit the ball, and that's why he was rarely an everyday player. Baltimore was the seventh major-league team he had played for. His real first name was Cyrus—his love for Cuban cigars was the reason for his nickname. Cig was Waddy's favorite because he looked like his uncle Burlton Richardson. A big, fun-loving man, Uncle Burl would always bring Waddy a treat when he came to visit. Unfortunately, Uncle Burl had been killed in a trac-tor accident three years before. The whole family, and Waddy most of all, missed Uncle Burl terribly. His only fault in the world, according to Waddy's father, was smoking foul-smelling cigars. "I just don't see the need of it," he said.

Waddy realized he could probably watch the game on TV. He quickly moved to the set, finally figured how to work the remote, and flipped around until—wow!—there it was. Waddy could see who was batting on the TV, then run to the window and view the actual "game board" figure for real. Then back to the TV to watch him bat. Suddenly this was better than even a sleepover or a poker game or anything else Waddy could think of.

He then turned off the overhead light so the game, both live and televised, would be more vivid. And it was. After running back and forth from window to TV for a couple of innings, Waddy was sweating. Then he remembered why he had parted the drapes in the first place. To open the window and get some air, which now he did. He would close the window before he went to bed, especially since Mr. Bernard would be waking him up in the morning.

Tonight, the Orioles were playing the Detroit Tigers.

The score had been tied one to one when Waddy first turned on the TV. But now, in the seventh inning, the Tigers had jumped ahead *six* to one. The only good thing about that was Cig *might* get to pinch-hit. Sure enough, in the bottom of the eighth, Waddy's hero came out to bat for the Orioles pitcher. Waddy was ecstatic. There was Cig filling up the twenty-seven-inch screen (the Richardsons' TV was only fifteen inches) and in color yet.

Waddy ran from the TV to the window and back again. Now he could say he had actually seen Cig Cartwright in person, even if not very close. The camera zoomed in on Cig as Waddy returned to the screen. For all the world, he looked exactly like Uncle Burl.

Cig took a couple of practice swings, then dug in against pitcher Milt Moraine of the Tigers. Moraine had a reputation of "doing things" to the ball to make it harder to hit. *Doctoring the ball* was the term Waddy had seen in the newspaper. Waddy knew more about sports than most of his buddies, since he had to read the papers to get the scores and the accounts of the games instead of watching ESPN and other sports channels. The papers gave more details, and Waddy could reread them as much as he wanted.

Cig Cartwright was quickly behind in the count, no balls and two strikes. He had swung mightily at two pitches that appeared to drop at least a foot the moment they reached the plate. After the second swing, Cig stepped out of the box and laughed and pointed at Moraine as though he knew the pitcher was doctoring the ball. Moraine just grinned and pointed back as if to say, "I don't need to doctor the ball to strike *you* out, you big ape." Then Moraine wound up and fired again. Once more the ball dropped like a lead weight when it reached the plate. But this time Cig anticipated the unusual action of the horsehide. He lowered his bat to meet the ball, and with a swing as powerful as when Uncle Burl had once chopped down a six-foot white pine for a Christmas tree with a single blow, Cig Cartwright clobbered the ball.

For a moment, there was hardly a movement. The stadium was quiet. Cig stood at home plate watching the flight of the ball. Usually, this action would be a sign of disrespect for the opposing pitcher. But there was no mockery on Cig's face. Almost in slow motion, the catcher rose and stood beside Cig. The umpire took off his mask and moved slightly to his left. All three, along with the pitcher, the fielders, both dugouts, and thirty thousand fans in the stands, watched with awe the launching of the ball from Cig's herculean clout.

Quickly, Waddy rushed to the window to witness the spectacle, live with his very own eyes. Suddenly the stands erupted with a mighty roar. Waddy scrambled back to the TV set to watch Cig circle the bases. The camera then zoomed to the outfield stands over which the ball had flown, still going up and up, higher and higher. All the spectators were turned with their backs to the field trying to find the small white orb against the dark sky.

"What a shot! This could be one for the record books," Waddy heard the announcer exult as the cheers of the throng grew even louder. Just at that moment, Waddy heard another sound—a "whooshing" noise— no more than a few inches from his ear. He spun around but saw nothing. Of course, the room was still dark, except for the TV and the faint glow from the lights of the city outside the window.

What was the noise? Where could it have come from? Then, a moment later, it registered.

He had heard that very same sound before. Flying bats made it when they entered the barn back on the farm. "Oh no," he moaned. If there was one thing

Waddy hated worse than rats, it was bats! He quickly closed the window, turned on the lights, and threw frantic glances about the room in search of the intruder. He'd forgotten all about the game and Cig's tremendous blow, even though the announcer was still shouting and estimating the home run to be at least six hundred feet or more. Waddy had to get that bat out of there. He searched the room, the bathroom, the closet, under the bed, everywhere. Nothing. The only hope was to turn off all the lights and the TV and reopen the window, which he did, and hope the bat would find its way out again.

Without even taking off his clothes and putting on his pajamas, Waddy slowly and quietly lay down on the bed. His pillow was directly in line with the window, so that he could at least see the bat fly away. If it ever did.

Waddy was suddenly aware of a lump underneath his pillow. He lay very, very still. Of course. That was it. The lump *had* to be the bat! It had flown right through the window, and, perhaps, before it could stop, it had gotten caught under the pillow. Maybe it had knocked itself out. Or maybe not. At that moment, Waddy was sure he felt it move.

There was only one thing to do. Take the pillow, double it up around the bat, hold the pillow out the window, shake the bat free, then slam the window shut.

Slowly and methodically, Waddy began to carry out his plan. Finally, when he was at the window, he breathed a deep sigh of relief. It was almost over. Almost. But there was one thing that concerned him. The lump in the pillow seemed to be a bit bigger than a bat. And harder. Waddy had never held a bat in his hands, and he never planned to. But wouldn't a bat be a little squishy?

Something kept Waddy from unfolding the pillow and letting go of the bat. If it *was* a bat. What if it was something else? Something that somebody left behind, maybe. But what? Wait. When Uncle Burl would stay at Waddy's house, he always put his *billfold* under his pillow at night.

What if the lump was somebody's billfold? With his heart in his throat, Waddy slowly unfolded the pillow and opened it. To his great relief, all he heard was a small thud on the carpet below. If it *was* a bat, it had flown into its last barn.

Waddy ran to the light switch, flicked it on, and saw the object on the floor. It was a baseball. Had somebody left a baseball under the pillow?

He walked almost on tiptoe to the ball, gingerly picked it up, and read the lettering:

RAWLINGS

• *Official Ball* •

AMERICAN LEAGUE

BOBBY BROWN PRES.

CUSHIONED CORK CENTER

RO-A

The last three letters of *League* and all of *Pres.* were faded, as if someone had tried to rub them out with sandpaper. Waddy studied the ball for a long time. Suddenly he remembered the game, and he looked out toward the stadium. But the field was empty, even though the lights were still on. In the time he had tried to find and capture the bat, the game had ended.

He turned the TV back on. All three local stations were covering the same story—a sports story about what might be the longest home run ever hit in the history of baseball. Camera crews roamed the streets and alleys behind the center-field stands where people were running this way and that, as though looking for something.

Waddy went to the window and saw a handful of people moving about in the street below. Were they looking for the ball? Could it possibly have come this far? Just then, a police car, its red light flashing, slowly moved into the area and shooed the people away.

Waddy pushed the window shut and turned back to the TV. A reporter was interviewing pitcher Milt Moraine, who had already showered and dressed. "Milt, are you saying you can positively identify the ball that Cig Cartwright hit tonight?" asked the reporter.

"That's right." Moraine nodded, putting a stick of gum into his mouth.

"Are you possibly admitting that you might have 'doctored' the ball in some way before you pitched it to Cig?"

"I'm admitting nothing. But I do know that tomorrow two or three hundred people are going to come to the Orioles office with an official American League baseball and say, 'Here's the ball Cig Cartwright hit for a home run last night. I found it all the way up on such-and-such street. Or in Mrs. So-and-So's backyard. Or under this or that overpass.' But I'm the only one who'll know which is the real ball."

"And you're willing to go to the Orioles office and verify it?"

"Why not?" replied Moraine as he took out a small metal nail file and began working on his nails. "Look." He chuckled. "I'm not proud to be the one who served up that dinger, but it *is* nice to be a small part of history. So, when we know where that ball was found, we'll know if Cig Cartwright hit the longest home run ever here tonight."

"And, as we said before," intoned the reporter, "the current record is Mickey Mantle's six-hundred-and-thirty-four-foot home run on September tenth, 1960, against these same Detroit Tigers. At least that's what the *Guinness Book of World Records* says."

"Right," the pitcher concurred. "Anyway, Cartwright's an old friend of mine. We played on the same minor-league team together. So, if this is a new record, I need to certify the home run by identifying the ball. It's my responsibility to Cig—and to the integrity of the game." He then looked directly into the camera and warned, "Just remember, fans, if you ain't got the ball, don't bother to call the Orioles office. 'Cause I'll know."

"Thank you, Milt," said the reporter, "and by the way,

congratulations on being the winning pitcher tonight."

"Oh yeah." Moraine smiled. "We *did* win, didn't we. I almost forgot." He put the nail file back into his pocket and walked away.

"Remember, fans," cautioned the reporter, looking into the camera, "as Milt Moraine so poetically put it, 'If you ain't got the ball, don't bother to call.' But if you do, here's the number, and we'll keep it posted at the bottom of the screen throughout the newscast." He then gave the phone number, which also appeared on the TV.

"Needless to say," he continued, "this ball will be worth a lot of money to the finder. The Orioles—and Major League Baseball—simply want to validate the ball and the location where it was found to determine how far it was hit. If our estimation is correct, it will set a new world record. Even if you don't come forward immediately, please do call the number below after you have consulted with your attorney or accountant or"— he added with a wink—"eBay. This is Marv Mellencamp, saying s'long from Camden Yard on this historic evening."

Waddy stared at the ball again, particularly at the faded letters—letters that might have been rubbed partially away with sandpaper. Or perhaps, it began to dawn on Waddy, by a nail file. A nail file that had been hidden in a pitcher's cap or glove during a game. And only that pitcher would know exactly which letters had been affected.

Practically holding his breath, and with his heart pounding, Waddy grabbed a pen and a piece of stationery from the desk in his room and wrote down the number at the bottom of the screen. For he realized that he held in his hand perhaps the most valuable object in the history of baseball—or maybe even all of sports.

Whom should he tell first? One of his buddies? A teacher? Should he call the Orioles office right now? Should he not say anything about it till he got home? Waddy knew the events of this night could change his life forever. But after some thinking, he wasn't sure that would be a good thing. What if he and his family got a whole lot of money for the ball? Would his father stop being a farmer? Would they leave the house they were in? Would they move away from Wonder?

Maybe, just maybe, he should keep quiet about the whole thing. Put the ball in his chest of drawers at home, just look at it from time to time and know he had the greatest sports souvenir that ever was. But then the voice of Milt Moraine echoed in his ear: *It's my responsibility to Cig—and to the integrity of the game.*

Waddy thought about it for a few minutes, then knew what he had to do. If Cig Cartwright had indeed hit the longest home run ever, Waddy owed it to him— and to the game—to let everybody know that he had the ball and where he found it. And he wouldn't sell it either. He would give it to the Hall of Fame. He had always wanted to see the Hall of Fame. And maybe they would take his family there and put them up in a swanky hotel. And maybe they could even get their picture taken with Cig Cartwright. Wouldn't that be something?

Yes, that's what he would do. He wouldn't wake Mr. Bernard up tonight, but first thing tomorrow morning, he would tell him the whole story. Mr. Bernard would know, of course, that Waddy had opened the window. But he hoped the principal would still think he was trustworthy and had a "good name," which, he was pretty sure, *is* better than great riches. And with that, Wadleigh Harvey Richardson III finally fell asleep.

OH, BROTHER

I see you,
big brother.

BY Sandy Asher

Clearly.

Oh, yes.

You don't say much.
Not to me, anyway.

You're just going "out,"
going "'round the corner,"
going "with some guys."
Going, going,
on the go.

But never gone.
Not for me, anyway.

You're on your own,
But I've never known
a single day
without you in it.

And always
birthdays,
grades,
and giant steps ahead.

Always
taller,
tougher,
running faster,
jumping higher.

Punching harder, too.

You don't care
because you don't know
because you don't notice
that

I

am

growing

up.

Catching on.

Closing in.

Any day now,
you will
suddenly
turn
and see me.

Clearly.

Gaining on you,
big brother.

Oh, yes.

WATERMELON KISSES

BY José Cruz González

• CHARACTERS •

Quetzal (Ket-zal) is a nine-year-old Latino boy. Quetzal is an ancient Aztec name that means "Feather." He is the older brother to Tlaloc.

Tlaloc (Tla-lok) is a seven-year-old Latino boy. Tlaloc is also an ancient Aztec name that means "Rain God."

• TIME •

A summer's day.

• PLACE •

The front porch steps to an old house.

• WORDS IN SPANISH •

Papá (Pa-paah!): "Dad."

Tonto (Tone-toe): "Dummy."

Mamá (Ma-maah!): "Mom."

• AT RISE •

Two Latino boys, Quetzal and Tlaloc, are seated eating watermelon. Alongside them rest a rake and a hoe. A lawn mower is heard in the background.

QUETZAL

Don't eat the watermelon seeds, *Tlaloc*.

TLALOC

Why not?

QUETZAL

'Cause they go into your tummy and get planted.

TLALOC

Huh?

QUETZAL

Yeah, they get planted in your stomach and then green vines start to rise up through your throat and ears and spill out everywhere.

TLALOC

Nah-uh!

QUETZAL

Ah-huh! Pretty soon you can't hear 'cause you got vines growing out of your ears and you can't talk 'cause you got a watermelon growing on your chin.

TLALOC

For reals?

QUETZAL

For reals, little brother!
(Tlaloc accidentally swallows one, maybe even two watermelon seeds.)

TLALOC

I think I ate a watermelon seed, *Quetzal.*
(The lawn mower is heard shutting off.)

QUETZAL

Why does *Papá* always wait until the grass is a foot high before cutting it?

TLALOC

Did you hear me? I think I ate a watermelon seed, maybe two.

QUETZAL

You're supposed to spit them out, *Tonto.*

TLALOC

Hey, I didn't know! Nobody told me!

QUETZAL

You'll be okay. Just don't get kissed by a girl.

TLALOC

What?

(The lawn mower is heard starting up.)

QUETZAL

Nothing happens unless a girl kisses you.

TLALOC

I don't understand.

QUETZAL

Do I have to explain everything to you? Uh-oh, start raking!

TLALOC

Huh?

QUETZAL

Papá is giving us the eyebrow look. Get busy!
(Quetzal and Tlaloc work in the yard. Tlaloc turns to his brother.)

TLALOC

What if *Mamá* kissed me?

QUETZAL

She kissed you?

TLALOC

Yeah, on my cheek before she went to the store.

QUETZAL

Oh, man.

TLALOC

What?

QUETZAL

She activated it.

TLALOC

Act-a-what?

QUETZAL

When a girl kisses you—

TLALOC

But *Mamá's* not a girl.

QUETZAL

It doesn't matter. She used to be a girl. Now the seeds you ate are going to grow 'cause you got kissed.

TLALOC

You mean I'm going to have a watermelon growing on my chin?

QUETZAL

I told you not to eat the seeds.

(The lawn mower is heard stopping again.)

Papá's face is getting red again. He looks like a tomato.

(A worried Tlaloc drops his rake to the ground. He starts to hurry off as…)

QUETZAL

What are you doing?

TLALOC

I'm telling *Papá* I got a watermelon growing out of my stomach!

QUETZAL

You better not!

TLALOC

Why?

QUETZAL

'Cause he's going to be mad at you 'cause you got a kiss. Did you notice that *Mamá* didn't kiss him when she left?

TLALOC

No.

QUETZAL

Well, I did. *Papá's* in the doghouse 'cause he didn't mow the lawn when he was supposed to.

TLALOC

Quetzal, I don't want a watermelon growing on my chin!

QUETZAL

Okay, pipe down! *Papá* will hear you.

TLALOC

Are you going to help me?

QUETZAL

Yeah, I'll think of something.
(The lawn mower is heard starting up again.)

TLALOC

Well?

QUETZAL

Okay, stick your finger down your throat.

TLALOC

Why?

QUETZAL

You want those seeds out, right?

TLALOC

Yeah, but—

QUETZAL

There's no buts, just do it.

TLALOC

PAPÁ!

QUETZAL

Fine! You don't have to stick your finger down your throat.

TLALOC

Are you making this up?

QUETZAL

Why would I make this up?

TLALOC

I don't know.

QUETZAL

I'm your big brother. Big brothers never lie.
(Quetzal sits on the porch steps.)

Oh, man, it's so hot. I'm going to eat some more watermelon. Want some?

TLALOC
No way!

QUETZAL
Guess I'll have to eat it all myself.

TLALOC
Well?

QUETZAL
How much money you got?

TLALOC
I got a dollar.

QUETZAL
A whole dollar?

TLALOC
Yeah.
(*Tlaloc pulls a dollar from his pocket to show Quetzal.*)

QUETZAL
When did you get a whole dollar?

TLALOC

Mamá gave it to me 'cause I did my chores and yours all week.

QUETZAL

I was going to do them.

TLALOC

I'm saving my dollar in my new piggy bank.

QUETZAL

Half of that dollar is mine, you know.

TLALOC

Mamá said you'd say that.

QUETZAL

She did?

TLALOC

Ah-huh.
(*Quetzal looks closely at Tlaloc's face.*)
What?

QUETZAL

It's nothing. I thought I saw something green.
(*The lawn mower is heard stopping again.*)
Don't look, but *Papá's* kicking the lawn mower.

TLALOC

Quetzal, tell me what I got to do?

QUETZAL

The only way to stop a watermelon seed from growing is to spend that dollar.

TLALOC

No.

QUETZAL

Yeah, you have to go to the corner store and buy ice cream.

TLALOC

Ice cream?

QUETZAL

Why do you always repeat everything I say?

TLALOC

'Cause you mumble!

QUETZAL

No, I don't!

TLALOC

Yes, you do!

QUETZAL

Fine!

(Long pause. Quetzal doesn't say a word.)

TLALOC

Okay, you don't mumble.

(Quetzal still doesn't say a word.)

Please!

QUETZAL

You buy an ice cream and eat it. The cold will freeze the seed and stop it from growing.

TLALOC

For reals?

QUETZAL

For reals. Why would I make this up? What would I have to gain?

TLALOC

I don't know.

(Tlaloc thinks for a moment. The lawn mower starts up again.)

Quetzal, *Papá* won't let me go to the store by myself.

QUETZAL
I'll go with you.

TLALOC
You will?

QUETZAL
Yeah, but—

TLALOC
What?

QUETZAL
You'll have to buy me an ice cream, too.

TLALOC
For reals?
(Quetzal nods his head in agreement. Tlaloc looks at his dollar. Then at his brother.)

TLALOC
Okay.

QUETZAL
Great, let's go!

TLALOC
Quetzal?

QUETZAL

Yeah?

TLALOC

If I ever find out you lied to me, I'm going to climb up into your bunk when you're asleep and hit you real hard.

QUETZAL

You wouldn't do that, would you?
(Tlaloc just shrugs his shoulders.)

That's not right. You shouldn't say such a thing.

TLALOC

I didn't say anything.

QUETZAL

I look out for you. I'm taking you to the store.

TLALOC

I know you're scared of the night.

QUETZAL

No, I'm not.

TLALOC

Then why do you keep taking my teddy bear?
(Tlaloc embraces the rake tightly.)

QUETZAL

'Cause he makes a good pillow!

TLALOC

If I ever find out, you better learn to sleep with one eye open, big brother.

QUETZAL

You're joking, right? Right?
(*Tlaloc shrugs his shoulders once more. The lawn mower stops again.*)

PAPÁ!
(*Quetzal runs off. Tlaloc picks up a watermelon slice and eats it. End of play.*)

GOING FOR GOLD

BY Jane Yolen

I'll stand tall, gold around my neck,
Smile at the cheering crowd,
Cry a bit as the anthem plays,
And sing the words out loud.
I'll high-five every swim-mate,
Wave at all the fans,
Mouth "Hi, Mom!" very carefully
As the camera pans.
I'll be graceful in each interview,
My body hard and trim,
Can almost feel that medal now,
But first—must learn to swim.

TO SPEAK OR NOT TO SPEAK

BY Edwin Endlich

THE CLASSROOM

The blood is rushing out of my arm. This must be how it feels to be in a dungeon, when they chain your arms up. The sound in the room is also like a dungeon, people moaning and whimpering.

We all sit in Mr. Harper's classroom with our hands raised. He just asked an easy question that we all know. It's a give-away question for all of us who never get the hard ones.

He asked "What sport does Shaquille O'Neal play?" This is intended to get the guys who never answer anything right to feel good about themselves, and for the kids who never raise their hands to feel forced to. I have to raise my hand. Everyone in the room has theirs up. Of course I know the answer. I have Shaq's poster up in my room. But I'm scared to death that Mr. Harper will call on me. I have to at least look like I want to speak, though. Like everyone else I raise my arm high, propping it higher with my other arm, flickering my fingers.

Mr. Harper scans the room, holding out his massive arm, waiting to extend his finger to the lucky winner. He glares intensely, breathing heavily, as though he's choosing who he's going to carry from a burning building. He looks at Mark, who wears his soccer uniform to school even when he doesn't have a game, and I'm relieved. Mark never says anything. He's worse than I am. It's going to be okay. Then, as if willed by the gods, Mr. Harper turns to me. With my hand still waving wildly, I give Mr. Harper a look, a desperate glance. Don't call on me — don't you dare call on me.

But I see his finger start to unfurl from his fist. I see my own face in the reflection of his large glasses. I'm horrified. The hands in the room fall to their desks with a loud *thud*.

I know the answer. I know this. It's easy. Showtime. Breathe. Blow a little air out of your lips to get the flow going. Just put your voice on the air going through your lips. That's all you have to do. Do it.

Nothing. Absolutely nothing. It's not going to happen. I'm not going to get the word *basketball* out.

See, I'm a stutterer. I know what I want to say, but when I open my mouth, things tend to come out all wrong. Either the words skip, like: st st st st stutter. Or I have to drag it out, like: Ssssssssstututer. Then, to make it worse, when I try really hard to say something and it won't come out, the muscles in my mouth start working like crazy, and I can't get them to stop. It looks like I'm chewing a huge piece of gum.

I'm faced with a choice now. I could sit here and wait for Greg to laugh and imitate me by going "bbbbbb…bbbbbbb." That usually gets a laugh from the class. I laugh, too. I learned the more you laugh along with someone making fun of you, and just shake your head in an "I know…I know" way, the easier it is to look normal.

So, I make my choice. Today I will take the high road. I will not be laughed at for stuttering. I say the answer, loud and clear: "Hockey." I proclaim that Shaquille O'Neal plays hockey. I know it's wrong. Who doesn't? But "hockey" is a lot easier to say than "basketball." "Hockey" will come out.

Now that gets a laugh. I put my head on my desk. Why does it have to start with a *B*? Why can't it be called yasketball, or sasketball? I can say those. I hate hard consonants. Everyone else in this class probably hates brussels sprouts or wearing a suit, but I hate hard consonants more than anything. Sometimes that means not having what I want. On the lunch line, if I want pepperoni pizza, I'll order a ham sandwich. When my mom takes me shopping and I see a sweater, I say I want it in yellow, even though I really want it in black.

THE THERAPIST'S OFFICE

I'm sitting in a room that looks like a kid's playroom. There are toys for preschoolers everywhere, so I feel like I'm a baby. I sit across from my speech therapist, who is holding a weird device in her hands. She calls it a "talking machine." It's a shiny black box that looks like a car battery.

Out of the top snakes a long black cord that leads to the largest headphones you can imagine, like the kind that construction workers use to drown out the noise of a jackhammer.

She smiles as she puts the headphones on me. I'm not smiling. The headphones are too tight, pressing against my head. I feel like I'm being interrogated by the secret police, and now they're going to torture me. They want me to talk.

She puts a book in front of me and motions for me to start reading. I start to read, and I hear a strange echo in my ears, like I'm yelling into the Grand Canyon. The headphones play back what I just said half a second ago. At first I think it's broken, but then I realize that the playback is forcing me to read half as fast as I normally do. The echo somehow slows me down, forcing…me…to…say…everything…really…slowly. After five minutes I feel like I'm underwater. I'm trapped inside the sounds of my own words, and I can't get out. I rip off the headphones.

My therapist looks at me and frowns. She says that the machine can help me. She says this big one is for therapy, but they are making smaller ones that I could wear all the time.

All the time? I can't wear that all the time. Can you

imagine? I'll be half man, half machine. Like Darth Vader.

Now, I love Darth Vader, so I'd be okay with it if people were afraid of me and I got a cape out of the deal. But I keep thinking about how everyone would look at me. Right now people need about a minute or two talking to me to know that there's something wrong. But if I have to wear this machine, people from across the Atlantic will be able to see that I have a weird problem. People might think that someone else was telling me what to say. People will think I'm a cyborg.

As cool as that may sound, it's not what I want. I just want to be a normal kid. And a machine around my neck will be a neon sign announcing that I'm not normal.

MY ROOM

I run off the bus and go up the stairs to my room. This is the one place I don't stutter. It's the strangest thing: when I go into my room, I feel like I've walked through a portal to a parallel universe, a place where I can talk. No matter what I want to say, when I'm alone in my room, I can say it. I spend hours and hours reenacting the entire day, the day when I *talked.* I answer a teacher's question. I stand up for myself in front of Greg. I talk to girls. I can't fall asleep unless I've gone through my day and said everything I would have if I could. My mom calls me to come down for dinner. I pretend not to hear her. I'm not done yet.

THE CHOIR ROOM

It is the first day of a new class. Choir. It's mandatory to take one singing class, and I'm trying to hide as far as possible in the back. I feel like I'm in a holding pen for cattle, packed in, not knowing what to do. The room is full of kids like me, who have no interest in singing "A Whole New World." The choir teacher, Mr. Ebert, comes in and starts the class. Mr. Ebert is a large man with the highest voice I've ever heard. He talks about singing from the diaphragm, and who is an alto, tenor, or soprano. Finally we start, most of us laughing the whole time. After a few verses, I realize I'm not stuttering when I sing. I must be using another part of my brain or maybe my mouth does something different when I sing. I'm getting through words I can never say. I can't believe it.

THE THERAPIST'S OFFICE, AGAIN

I'm back in the playpen, and I tell my therapist what happened. She says that there are people who can speak fluently when the words are sung or prepared. Like actors. Now, I know a lot of famous people who stutter, but I didn't know that learning what an actor does can actually help you speak fluently. She tells me about Marilyn Monroe, Bruce Willis, and James Earl Jones. All were stutterers, but used scripts and acting techniques to overcome their speech impediments. Wait a minute. Are you telling me that James Earl Jones, *Darth Vader*, stutters? Why didn't anyone ever tell me this before?! This is a sign.

THE HALLWAY

I'm looking at the poster taped up against the glass of the trophy case. Auditions for the school musical are in two weeks. I saw the same poster last year, but never thought about it. I always had an image of myself onstage:

"To bbbb...bbb be...or not to...bbb bbbb. It's a tough question, okay?"

* * *

But now I have a new image. I'm onstage, and talking. Everyone is listening to me. Hearing every perfect word. And it's not like I've never acted before. I do it every day in my room. I've got to give it a shot. I feel my stuttering is getting worse. About a month ago I started having trouble saying my own name.

THE AUDITION ROOM

The line for auditions wraps around the auditorium. I try to read over my monologue and my song lyrics one more time, but my hands are shaking too much. People keep looking at me. Someone tries to cut into line behind me. I hear them whisper that they want to audition after me, so they look better. Great. Thanks.

I spent the past two weeks practicing nonstop. I memorized the monologue backward and forward. I performed it in my room for hours, and I even went over it with my therapist. We worked through some of the hard parts with the talking machine. It helped me slow down, take my time.

There's a window that looks into the room, and everyone is pressed against it, looking in at the people auditioning. The window is all fogged from our breath, so we have to wipe it with our shirts.

I walk into the audition room and see Mr. Ebert sitting at the piano. He smiles at me. Also in the room are the director and her assistant, who never stops writing. The director tells me to start my monologue. Showtime. Breathe. Blow a little air out of your lips to get the flow going. Just put your voice on the air going through your lips. Do it.

Nothing.

I've got too many thoughts in my head. I count the Bs and the Ks and the Ds in the monologue. There's no way I can get past them. They're like huge trees that fell on the road. What was I thinking? I should just leave now, before I embarrass myself.

I close my eyes. I hear the squeaking of people wiping away the fog on the window. I hear the assistant write something down. I imagine the black box around my neck, the headphones pressing against my head. I picture myself in my room with a million locks on the door so I never have to talk to anyone.

Stop. Breathe. That's not the life I want. And if I want it to be different, I'm going to do something about it. Right now. What would Darth Vader do? I bet he practiced what he was going to say the night before, in his bedroom. He would warm up his voice using acting techniques, like I did. He'd get a little help from the talking machine he got from his evil speech therapist. He would walk into this room, hold his head high, and talk. Darth Vader knows he can do it. I can, too.

I take a breath, open my eyes, and look up.

"I'm ready," I say.

THE HALLWAY

Everyone clamors around the posting of the cast. I don't expect much. Maybe a chorus part. I walk up and people start patting me on the back. Were they impressed that I tried out? Thanks, I guess. I look up and see the posting. I got a part. And not a small one either. I keep looking at the list, making sure I'm not seeing things.

This is unbelievable. I bet the director and her assistant don't know I stutter. I didn't once during the whole audition. I'm sure they'll find out from someone, but maybe they'll say, "Really? I didn't notice. It's obviously not a big deal."

It's not a big deal.

Wait. This could be bad. What if I just had a good day? What if this magic potion wears off and I can't act without stuttering? What if at midnight, I turn into a pumpkin?

The whole play will be ruined. It'll all be my fault. This could be very bad.

There is a hand on my shoulder. It's Mr. Ebert. With his high voice he says, "You were great. Don't worry; I'll help you if you need it. You'll do fine."

THE STAGE

It's my turn to bow. I walk to the front of the stage. This is it. The show is over. Not one stutter. No more worries. The cast grabs hands, and I imagine my therapist is here, and Mr. Harper, and Mr. Ebert, all part of this bow. Maybe Darth Vader, too.

I hold my head up high. I know that I haven't cured anything, and I'm not planning on being a movie star. That's not why I'm proud. I'm proud because I fought for it. This may not be the last time I battle with stuttering. But I'll always know that one time, I won.

FAMILY MEETING

BY Bill C. Davis

The last family meeting we had was about where to have dinner.

So now that my dad is calling *this* family meeting I'm not thinking much of it. But he looks kind of white—no blood in his face—so I wonder what's up. We live in Georgia, and if you're white your face is either red or tan. My dad's face is usually tan—but not now for some reason.

My stepmom has her arms folded and she's sitting in that chair I can't stand. It's a plaid chair that rocks on hidden springs. I can't tell whether *she's* rocking the chair or the chair is rocking her. She's kind of big—not fat really; just…big…is all I can say. But she's rocking like she doesn't know she's rocking. She's looking down as if she's mad at a spot on the floor—or scared of it.

My little brother, Meric, is in the family meeting—well, the truth is, Meric is my *half* brother. My dad doesn't like me calling him that, but that's what he is. My older brother, Sam, is not at the meeting. He's also my half brother, but I *never* call him that because he doesn't feel half. The family setup is complicated—not to me—but when I try to explain it to someone who just meets me, they get this weird look on their face. This is what I tell them:

My dad married *Sam's* mom when she got pregnant with Sam. They got divorced. And then he married *my* mom when she got pregnant with *me*. And then my mom—well…she died. I was two and half—it was pretty bad all around for everyone 'cause—you know—they all said she was so full of life and no one could ever imagine she, of all people, could ever…oh, you know—all that stuff people say. And then Dad had to marry my stepmom 'cause she got pregnant with *Meric*. That's when whoever I'm telling this gets that look on their face—like…"What?" It's not that they dislike my dad, they just wonder how that could happen three different times to one man in one life.

All I'm thinking as I'm waiting for this family meeting to get started is that I hope it's quick. I like taking my bike to my friend Ryan's house right around this time of day. His mom and dad have cocktail hour, and Ryan and I get some concoction we're allowed to make up—all fruit juice and soda.

So we're downstairs in a room that my mom tells her friends is a finished family room. Meric is sitting on the floor with his skinny legs all folded like taffy. I'm sitting on a bar stool and she's doing this rocking which is hypnotizing me—and my dad is standing.

I'm waiting for someone to speak, and I notice my dad's eyes are wet. I look away from him. I don't know why. Give him privacy, I guess, even though he's standing right there. Why are his eyes getting wet?

He didn't do this when he told me my grandpa died—my real mom's dad. Grandpa loved my mom—his daughter—more than he loved his other kids. He told me that—like a secret. She had named me after him—Kevin. So that was a major deal for him. After she died, he wanted to have me around him in the worst way. He wanted to do things for me—take care of me—like that was going to be his way to feel better or stay close to his daughter—my mom.

I'm thinking maybe this meeting is about my grandma

dying—Grandpa's wife—or "widow," I guess is what some people call her. But no—that doesn't make any sense. Dad got me *alone* to tell me about Grandpa dying—'cause it was important to me and it wouldn't have been important to Meric or Sam.

Sam started living with us back then. He's the one I talked about it with. He didn't mind talking about my grandpa dying because he knew what it felt like. I mean he loved the grandmother we shared—my dad's mom—more than anyone. He took care of her for a while when she was sick with empha-something—you know—she couldn't breathe hardly after smoking three packs of cigarettes a day for her whole life. Sam and I asked why she smoked so much, and she told us that they made it look so glamorous back when she was a girl.

Sam would have lived with her full-time if she had been in better shape, and they would have all let him. He stayed with her a lot anyway—out in the West, which is where she lived. Sam stayed there as much as they could both make it happen until she died. So he knew what I was feeling after I got the news about my grandpa.

Sam's real mom was a mess. She had a tattoo on the

top part of one of her boobs, and when he was a kid she would give him cough syrup to make him go to sleep. He had a lot of energy, and if she wanted to go out or have someone over—then she'd spoon him lots of cherry-flavored cough syrup and he'd be zonked and not a problem—to her.

Nobody liked that going on when they found out about it. I heard my mom wanted to adopt Sam, but—you know—she got sick pretty soon after having me, so that didn't work out.

Sam came to live with us because his mom said to my dad, "It's time you take over—I've done it for sixteen years, and yeah—you've had it rough, but nobody asked you to have fifty kids with fifty different women"…which was like way over the top, but I guess that's how you win an argument. Mess with the numbers.

My stepmom said okay about Sam living with us even though she said she had her hands full with Meric and me, which she didn't really. I think she thought maybe Sam would help—his being seventeen and that's almost like being a grown-up and I bet she thought he could babysit and then she could go to her meetings about crystals and psychics and some entity she was all into. Meric is still only eight, so he couldn't be left alone, and I'm twelve and supposedly not qualified to be a responsible sitter.

I knew Sam was not going to like taking orders from his second stepmom—my real mom being his first. *This* stepmom had rules like it was an army base or something, and she thought Sam was going to "benefit" from her basic training. But to Sam, any kind of orders from *her* looked like cough syrup, and he was through swallowing that.

It got so bad between Sam and my stepmom that one night while my dad was away she told Sam to get out. Sam said he wasn't going anywhere until his dad—the owner of the house—told him to leave. That made her almost purple. The red in her face was not from the Georgia heat—it was from inside her. Meric cracked up laughing. I got scared. Maybe Meric was scared, too. Laughing doesn't always mean you're having a great time.

Sam locked his door. She kicked it, letting him know that this is as much her house as it is "your father's house." She said that Sam was a chauvinist and no girl—not even the one he asked to the prom—would want anything to do with him.

Sam yelled back through the door while she was kicking it that the girl he asked said yes and that he was no chauvinist, he just knew what was right. Meric kept asking what a chauvinist was, and I didn't know how to tell him. I mean I knew, but sometimes it's hard to make it sound like a dictionary. Nothing sounds like a dictionary really.

Meric thought he was watching some reality show. I thought I was watching an earthquake. I didn't like it at all. I wanted her to shut up, but that's the last thing she'll do just as you wish she would.

We had to wait for five days for my dad to get back because Sam wouldn't take the phone. My stepmom held it out with my father on the other end, and Sam shook his head and said he was going to wait until our dad got back.

I talked to my dad on the phone when I was at Ryan's house and told him that it wasn't all Sam's fault and that you know how she gets sometimes and not that I'm being chauvinistic 'cause I'm not. When you get like that—kicking doors and screaming—it doesn't matter what sex you are—you're disqualified as far as I'm concerned. That's what I told my dad—he laughed, but you could tell it was stressing him big-time.

When my dad did get back, what he did and the way he was—well, it was the first time I thought I could really not like him. She wouldn't stop. He was tired. He talked to Sam *alone*, and they worked something out that I thought was not fair at all. But my dad couldn't take it—he was ready to jump out of a window, he said—not that there was any window in the house high enough to make that a big threat.

Anyway Sam's *real* mom—the one with the tattoo—well, she has a brother who lives twenty miles away from us. Not the swiftest guy in the world. He said he'd take Sam for a while until things cooled down, meaning until Sam was ready to apologize and do what was expected of him. None of it sounded too promising to me. I wanted to hear from my stepmom why Sam was moving out, and she gave me some line about Sam needing to get "inner clarity."

So Sam packed. I watched. He wouldn't let me say anything bad about Dad, which I tried to do because at that point I thought our stepmom couldn't help herself but Dad should have…Sam didn't let me finish the sentence.

I wanted to go tell my stepmom that Sam had lots of inner clarity if he could stop me from saying things he probably was thinking, like he wanted to protect me from having lousy thoughts—like he didn't want me to hate my dad—which I didn't. I just thought he should have been more loyal to us—his sons. I mean the truth is…I could be next.

And then the other thing my stepmom did was to call the mother of the girl that Sam was taking to the prom. I heard her tell the girl's mom what a problem he was and that she hoped Sam would get some perspective and enlightenment. And then went on to say what a filthy white trash creep Sam's uncle was, but that's where he had to stay until he found some—and she says it again—"inner clarity"—as if it was something *she* had.

And I know for sure the mother told her daughter that she was *not* going to let her go to any prom with some wacko kid who's living with a white trash uncle. Who knows what kind of car he'd pick her up in or how he would drive or if he would drink and drive or what the uncle might do to her if Sam brought her over to their house, which was in a part of town that she didn't even know about.

I know this girl told Sam that she couldn't go with him to the prom. I know that not because Sam told me, but because the girl called here and asked me for the number where Sam was, and just the way she asked you knew she wasn't going to call him to ask what kind of corsage she should get.

So after she did all that, I kept hearing my stepmom telling anyone who would listen how everything was so peaceful now that Sam was out of the house.

But now my dad is calling this family meeting, and if everything is so peaceful why is *she* rocking and why is *he* white?

My dad starts to say "Sam—" He stops. His voice sounds like a rope is wrapped around it. He tries again.

"Sam… shot himself."

I'm thinking this is no big deal. His redneck uncle probably had a gun or a rifle and it went off and Sam got hit in the toe and he'll be walking around with a stupid cast for a couple of months. But Dad says more.

"They found him in his car and… he shot himself— two nights ago."

Meric gets it faster than I do. He loses it—he starts to cry—then my dad cries, and my stepmom just rocks like she doesn't dare cry—like she knows it's not her right.

It's still not clear to me.

"He's dead?" I ask.

No one answers and that's my answer. I scream—like something in the night that wakes you up. I run upstairs to the kitchen. My dad yells after me.

"Kevin!" I don't care he's calling me.

I want to be in the kitchen—I don't know why. Food—life—I don't know.

My dad comes toward me—I don't want him to touch me at all until I know who I'm going to blame.

I yell, "A rifle? It was a rifle?"

"Yes."

"How could he—how do you aim a rifle at yourself in a car?"

I can't even picture it. "Stop," he tells me. Stop what? Stop thinking these questions? I'm not doing it on purpose. You can't tell me to stop.

My stepmom comes upstairs. She wants me to say what I'm thinking right now like she's plugged into some special cosmic current and she knows I better say I blame *her*. It's like she wants me to do it for my own good or some twisted noble crap like that. I'm not going to let her be that important. My dad tells her to stop—she insists. She knows I would say I blame her if

I could get my breath to say it. But I can't catch my breath. She never runs out of it.

This was Sam's decision, she says. He didn't have to do this—which I know she really better believe or she's going to be a bigger mess than she already is. She keeps going—she has to. His soul will find its way back here, she says. Dad finally tells her to stop talking like she's some priestess.

I run out of the house. He yells for me. I don't stop. I bet he's scared now that *I'm* going to do something crazy.

Someone has to pay for this, is what I'm thinking. Like I'm a law enforcer. I can't go back into the house until I know who's to blame. I start to run to Ryan's house—but no—I can't tell anyone yet. It doesn't sound right, even in my head.

He must have been crazy lonely. He must have felt like nobody even cared—like he was useless. *What am I doing here?* is all he must have been saying to himself. But everyone thinks that—don't they? Doesn't everyone think that? And then they come up with an answer one way or another? You don't need a rifle to answer that question, do you?

I can't stop wanting to blame someone. If she didn't throw him out—if Dad stood up to her—if the girl didn't listen to her mom and went to the prom with him no matter what—if his mother didn't give him cough syrup—if our grandmother didn't smoke just because they told her it was glamorous—if my mother didn't die.

I can't even picture what it must look like—what Sam looks like right this second.

I'm getting mad because why would he ever want me to be thinking about this—or why would he want me to have to try *not* to think about it. I don't want to be mad at him—it's cold to be mad at him—but I am. It feels better to be mad at him.

He didn't have to do this. Maybe he thought he did. But what about what *I* think? Why didn't he ask *me*? I would have told him to be really famous or rich and show them all—even Dad. Show them that they were stupid not to see how important he is—was.

He was so important and he didn't know—or didn't care—or couldn't take it—or couldn't figure out how to be important on his own.

I don't want my father to be too freaked out. I better get back to the family meeting. I don't care that I don't think of it as a family right now. I just think of it as a weird hotel.

So I'll go back. I'll let them say whatever they want. They can try to make me think whatever they want. But I know what I'm thinking now.

And if they ask me back at the family meeting what I'm thinking, I'm not going to tell them. But I'm thinking now I'm not going to be mad at Sam. I'm thinking I'll take Sam's unused years and *I'll* live them. Sam didn't want those years? I'll take them. My mom wanted her unused years more than anything. I'll take those years, too.

No one else needs to know what I'm doing. Sam and Mom will know—and I'll know. When you share a secret like that it makes you close to each other. It's like we'll have our own family meeting—every day. And just watch—I'm going to have so many great things to tell them for as long as I live.

THE ENEMY

BY John Urquhart

• CHARACTERS •

Aloysius P. Whitaker, nickname Ally, age twelve, a new volunteer in the Confederate Army, 15th Kentucky Brigade.

Corporal Billy Sackerton, a seasoned Confederate infantryman serving under General Bragg's command, 15th Kentucky Brigade.

Simon Trowbridge, age fifteen, serving in the Union Army of the Ohio, 5th Battery, Indiana Light Artillery.

• TIME •

October 8, 1862, Battle of Perryville, American Civil War.

• PLACE •

The top of a small hill, three miles east of Perryville, Kentucky, behind Confederate lines. An overturned supply wagon rests against a stone wall. Smoke fills the air. The remains of a campfire are nested against the wall.

• AT RISE •

In the distance are heard the sounds of men mustering for battle. Corporal Billy Sackerton enters. He has been wounded and walks with a limp. His makeshift uniform is disheveled and dirty. He wears a pistol at his belt and he carries a map in one hand. Ally follows. He wears an overcoat that is several sizes too big for him; a pair of suspenders hold up his pants, which also fit poorly. Ally has a stick that he carries like a rifle, swinging it from left to right as he advances. Sackerton stops, looks at his map, grunts, and peers into the distance.

ALLY

(sighting down the "barrel" of the stick) Pow!

CORPORAL

(turning on Ally) Private Whitaker!

ALLY

I was just practicing, Mr. Corporal. Like I was shooting Yankees!

CORPORAL

This isn't a game, Whitaker. You understand that?

ALLY

Yessir. I'm just ready to fight. That's all!

CORPORAL

I can see that. *(looking him over)* Where'd you get that coat, son?

ALLY

Belonged to my daddy.

CORPORAL

Mighty generous of your daddy, giving you a fine coat like that to fight in.

ALLY

It was my mama gave it to me. Daddy didn't need it anymore.

CORPORAL

How come?

ALLY

He got killed by the Yankees at Mumfordville.

CORPORAL

(pause) And so you joined up?

ALLY

Yessir.

CORPORAL

Well, I'm sorry about your father, boy. But I need you to settle down. There's a battle brewing.

ALLY

I know that, sir.

CORPORAL

And I'd be careful with that coat. A lotta men think that being at war gives them a license to steal. *(Reaches in his pocket.)* Here, take this. *(Hands Ally a small mirror.)*

ALLY

What is it?

CORPORAL

That's a signal mirror. Now let's get our bearings. *(Sackerton spreads his map out on the side of the wagon and studies it. Ally looks at his face in the mirror, looks at Sackerton, then picks up a piece of charcoal from the fire. Keeping one eye on the corporal, he uses the charcoal and the mirror to draw a beard on his chin.)*

CORPORAL

(looking up from the map) All right, Private Whitaker. This is gonna be your post.

ALLY

Way up here?

CORPORAL

Right behind that piece of rock wall.

ALLY

But Mr. Corporal, sir, I—

CORPORAL

(sternly) There's no better place for a lookout. You got a good view of the road and the river. Now take a look at this map.
(Ally goes to examine the map.)
That's the road to Frankfort. (points) You see it? Over there, by the creek?

ALLY

Yessir.

CORPORAL

You see them woods on the other side?
(Ally nods.)
Them woods is full of Yankee soldiers.

ALLY

Really! I don't see nuthin'.

CORPORAL

Trust me. Now, if you see any Union soldiers
moving out of those woods toward the back side of
this hill, General Bragg wants to know. That's what
the mirror's for. Point it in the sun and wiggle it.
We'll see it flashing down below, and I'll tell the
general. You understand, son?
*(Ally nods. As the corporal folds his map, Ally looks
down at the valley.)*

ALLY

Mr. Corporal, sir?

CORPORAL

What is it now, Private Whitaker?

ALLY

All the other men are lining up to fight.

CORPORAL

Yep. They'll be at it soon.

ALLY

Well, I joined up with the army so's I could fight.

CORPORAL

Most men do.

ALLY
- -

I can shoot. An' I'm good with horses. I can do most
anything, but you ain't even give me a gun yet. Or
a uniform.

CORPORAL
- -

If you want a uniform, son, you better join the
Union Army. They got plenty of uniforms. Better
food, too.

ALLY
- -

What's the point a' being a soldier if I ain't got a
gun and don't get to fight? I oughta be down there
with the rest of—

CORPORAL
- -

(*sharply*) Now you listen to me, *General* Whitaker,
and you listen good!
(*Ally snaps to attention.*)
You only been a soldier two days. I am not gonna
let a boy what ain't got any whiskers yet get within
range a' Yankee cannon.

ALLY
- -

(*sticking out his chin*) I got whiskers, sir! See! I ain't
no boy!
(*Sackerton pulls out a handkerchief, spits on it.*)

CORPORAL

Hold still!

(Sackerton wipes Ally's face and holds up the blackened handkerchief.)

I never seen whiskers rub off before.

(Ally remains at attention.)

How old *are* you, boy?

(A bugle sounds and shouting is heard. Sackerton starts and turns to look down the hill. The artillery begins to fire.)

CORPORAL

(shouting over the cannons) Now listen, Whitaker. The fight is on. You need to follow orders. *(Puts his hand on his pistol.)* You desert your post, I'll find you and shoot you myself. You hear me?

ALLY

I hear you good, Mr. Corporal, sir.

CORPORAL

And stop calling me sir. I ain't no officer. My name is Billy Sackerton.

ALLY

Yessir.

(The corporal shakes his head wearily and exits as quickly as his bad leg will allow.)

(mimicking Sackerton) "An' don't call me sir. I ain't no officer."

(Ally takes off his coat and hangs it on the wagon. Then he climbs up on the stone fence to watch the action in the valley below. Cannons volley in the distance.) There goes the cavalry. Whee-hoo! Look at 'em go. Get them Yankees! Go on! Go on, get 'em. *(Takes his hat off and slaps his leg.)* Go on, run 'em down! Look at those horses go. Giddyap! Beat it, you cowards. Get on back where you come from!

(Ally is so absorbed in the battle that he forgets his orders to watch the woods. He also fails to notice the entrance of Simon Trowbridge, a young soldier in the Union Army. Simon wears blue trousers, black boots, suspenders, and the top of his long johns. He carries a hat in his hand, but he is unarmed and out of breath from running up the hill. Simon leans against the wreck of the wagon, chest heaving. He looks back down the hill to see if he is being followed. Simon doesn't see Ally, but he does see the coat hanging on the wagon. Simon picks up the coat and examines it, then he slips it on. When Ally suddenly jumps up and shouts, Simon drops to his knees and ducks.)

ALLY

Yahoo! Look at those cowards run. Go get 'em,

Johnny Reb! Git those yellow-bellied Yanks! Chew
'em up and spit 'em out!

(As Ally stands on the rock wall, a rifle ball strikes the
rock at his feet.)

Whooaaa! What was that?

(Ally jumps to the ground, nearly landing on Simon.)

(to Simon) Did you see that? Somebody shot at me!
They almost hit me!

SIMON

You make a good target, standing up on top of a
wall like that.

ALLY

(coming to his senses) Hey, who are you? Where'd
you come from? (noticing the coat) And what are
you doing with my coat? Give me that!

(Ally dives at Simon, who stands up, revealing that he
is at least a head taller than Ally and perhaps twenty
pounds heavier. Ally grabs the coat and pulls on it.)

Take it off. It's my daddy's coat!

(Ally falls backward and pulls Simon down on top of
him.)

Owww! Get off me! You're squashing me!

(Simon easily gains control of Ally and sits astride his
chest.)

SIMON

If you'll hold still, I won't hurt you!

ALLY

Get off me, or I'll give you a licking! And take that coat off or else I'll—

(Simon puts his hand over Ally's mouth.)

SIMON

Now listen, will ya. I'm gonna let you up. But I don't wanna hurt you, okay! So settle down!

(Ally thrashes around, but he can't overcome Simon's weight advantage. Suddenly Simon leaps up, grabbing his hand.)

Owwww! You bit me!

(Ally scrambles to his feet and picks up his stick. He tries to hit Simon, who grabs it and holds on. The two boys begin to circle, each holding one end of the stick.)

What's the matter with you? I said I was gonna let you up!

ALLY

You take that coat off!

SIMON

I'll take it off, but you gotta promise you won't hit me with that stick.

ALLY

I ain't promising nothin'!

(They circle some more while Simon mulls it over.)

SIMON

Well, I'm gonna trust you anyhow. You hear me?

(Ally holds fast to the stick.)

I'm gonna let go now. Then I'm gonna take the coat off. Okay?

ALLY

Go on.

(Simon lets go. Then he slips the coat off and holds it out to Ally.)

SIMON

Here.

(Ally takes the coat and puts it on.)

It don't even fit you. Who'd you steal it from?

ALLY

I didn't steal it. And what are you doing up here? Did the corporal send you?

(The cannons fire, and Simon ducks. Ally looks over at the woods.)

You can tell him the Yanks ain't come out of the woods yet.

SIMON

(sitting) Nobody sent me.

ALLY

Well, whatcha doin' up here? Are you all right?

(Simon tries to ignore him.)

Are ya sick?

(Simon shakes his head no.)

Well, what's the matter, then?

(Simon stares at the ground.)

Don't you wanta be out there fighting?

(Simon looks up but doesn't speak.)

Ya aren't chicken, are ya?

SIMON

(firmly) I ain't no coward.

ALLY

Don't you wanta shoot some Yankees?

SIMON

No. I don't wanta shoot nobody.

ALLY

Whatcha mean?

SIMON

You ever shoot anybody?

ALLY

Well, no, I...

SIMON

You ever see anybody get shot?

ALLY

Not yet.

SIMON

How long you been a soldier? Not long, I reckon.

ALLY

Don't you get high-and-mighty with me or I'll whup ya again.

SIMON

(grinning) You know, you kinda remind me of my brother. He was bullheaded, just like you.

ALLY

I ain't bullheaded.

SIMON

That's what I mean. But the truth is, I never shot nobody neither. Not really. I was in the artillery corps. All we ever did was load up them big Parrot guns and shoot 'em off into nowhere. It was something. They're really loud, you know.

ALLY

I know.

SIMON

Then they sent me to the front lines, where we were shooting twelve-pounders at close range. *(pause)* That's when I saw what those cannons did. To the men. An' the horses.

ALLY

The horses? They shoot the horses?

SIMON

Sure they do. They shoot everything.
(Ally draws in the dirt with his stick.)

ALLY

I got a horse. Back home.

SIMON

What's its name?

ALLY

Sue. She's a paint.

SIMON

Soldiers took our horses. Then they burned down the barn. That's why we joined up. Me and my brother.

ALLY

Where's your brother?

SIMON

(Takes a deep breath.) He got himself killed. At Mumfordville.

ALLY

(after a long silence) My daddy died at Mumfordville. *(pause)* This is his coat.
(Ally and Simon sit together without speaking. The sounds of the battle continue in the valley. Ally studies Simon's uniform.)

Where'd you get that hat?

SIMON

The army give it to me. *(Holds up the hat.)* You want it? I don't need it anymore. I'm goin' home. Here. You take it. *(Tries to hand Ally his hat.)*

ALLY

That's a Yankee hat. *(backing off)* Are you? Are you a...a...?

SIMON

A what?

ALLY

A Yankee?

SIMON

I was born in Ohio. That makes me a Yankee, don't it?

ALLY

What I mean is, are you a Yankee soldier?

SIMON

(pause) Nope. I *used* to be a Yankee soldier. Now I'm just a Yankee. *(pause)* What are you going to do now? Are you gonna shoot me?

ALLY

I ain't got a gun.

SIMON

What's that stuff on your face?

ALLY

(wiping his chin) I fell down.

SIMON

How come you hate Yankees so bad?

ALLY

How come?

SIMON

Yeah. How come?

ALLY

'Cause you're the enemy, that's why. An' cause of my pa.

SIMON

You know, when I joined up, I thought I hated all the Johnny Rebs. They were the enemy. 'Cause of what they done to our farm. Now I don't hate nobody. Since my brother got killed, I just hate the war.

ALLY

(pause) What's your name?

SIMON

Simon. Simon Trowbridge. What's yours?

ALLY

Private Aloysius P. Whitaker. But you can call me Ally. Everybody does. You know what I'm gonna do, Simon?

SIMON

You're gonna shoot me. 'Cause I'm a Yankee.

ALLY

Nope. I'm gonna make you my prisoner. An' maybe I'll shoot you later.

SIMON

You can't shoot a prisoner. You know that, don't ya?
It's against the rules.

ALLY

What rules?

SIMON

The rules of war.

ALLY

Well, I can't shoot you anyway, can I? I got nuthin'
to shoot with.

CORPORAL

(from offstage) Whitaker! Private Whitaker!
(Simon hides. The corporal enters.)
There you are. We got to fall back. Let's go.

ALLY

What for? We was winnin'.

CORPORAL

An' now we ain't. The Yankees flanked us, and we're
retreating to the other side of the creek. General
Bragg's orders.

ALLY

(glancing at Simon's hiding place) What about
prisoners, sir?

CORPORAL

We ain't taking none.

ALLY

What do you mean, sir?

CORPORAL

There's no time to take prisoners when your army's retreating. You see any Yankees, you shoot 'em.

ALLY

But, Mr. Corporal, sir, you haven't given me a gun.

CORPORAL

Then you tell me, an' I'll shoot 'em for ya.

ALLY

Yessir.

CORPORAL

You seen any Yankee soldiers? *(pause)* Well?

ALLY

(pause) Nossir. Nary a one.
(*They exit as the sound of cannon fire fills the air.*)

TWELVE

BY Jaime Adoff

Twelve years old and my rhymes keep me sane

twelve years old, I see bullets and brains

twelve years old, and my story's been told...

Anything can happen when you're twelve years old.

Dad went to the desert before I was born.

Gulf war fighter in the desert storm.

Came back sick/now he can't get paid.

He used to love life

now he loves hate.

So hard on us livin' hand to mouth.

So hard on me, too much screamin' and shouts...

Tryin' so hard in school for grades

tryin' so hard for a life

every day.
Lookin' out my window watch dealers deal death
lookin' out my window, at all the last breaths...

Twelve years old and my rhymes keep me sane
twelve years old, I see bullets and brains
twelve years old, and my story's been told...
Anything can happen when you're twelve years old.

Try to be the man
when I'm only a kid
Try to do something
to help, to give.
So much temptation to get in the game
hustlin' and stealin' is easy—it's fame.
So far so good/Mom always says
so far so good/'cause I'm not dead
so far we'll see what the future brings
you gotta play ball or rap or sing
you gotta play ball or rap or sing...

TV babysitter dopin' my mind
Drainin' my smarts/makin' me blind.
Wanna be more than what they say I can be;

A doctor, a lawyer, a teacher,
free...

Twelve years old and my rhymes keep me sane
twelve years old, I see bullets and brains
twelve years old, and my story's been told...
Anything can happen when you're twelve years old.

I'm no poet or prophet/I'm just a kid
Writin' down what happens
every day that I live.
Hopin' things change but my days could be few.
Mom would be sad if I made the news...
sure would be sad if I made the news...

Twelve years old and my rhymes keep me sane
twelve years old, I see bullets and brains
twelve years old, has my story been told?

Everything can happen
when you're twelve years old.

LANKY BOYS WITH CARS

BY Ron Koertge

• CHARACTERS •

Dax: Twelve years old. Cargo pants, black T-shirt with a band's name on it. Stocky.

Josh: Also twelve. Spiky-haired. Jeans and a long-sleeved cotton shirt of good quality.

Carol: Dax's mom. Short hair. Very fit, wearing Nike warm-ups. Everything matches.

• TIME •

The present. An afternoon rehearsal.

• PLACE •

Backstage in a very small theater.

• AT RISE •

Two boys, Dax and Josh, both wearing angel wings, clearly handmade. Things around them have a makeshift look, as if the space is sometimes used for storage. Noises offstage suggest that they're not alone. Dax has a script, Josh a script and a book. Restless, they settle finally, Josh sitting up on a small table, Dax in a straight-backed chair.

DAX

Do you think Cooper Armstrong did all the stuff he says with Amber Franklin?

JOSH

There's no way.

DAX

What if I told Cooper you said he was a liar?

JOSH

Go ahead.

DAX

He'd kick your butt if I did.

JOSH

Is that what you want? For somebody to kick my butt?

DAX

I'm just saying. *(Then he looks at the script he's worrying and frowns as he quotes.)* "Their limbs are inordinately fair"?

JOSH

It means good-looking. Their legs and arms are good-looking.

DAX

How do you know that?

JOSH

I looked it up.

DAX

(sarcastically) You would.

JOSH

Hey, I'm doing you a favor. You begged me to be in your mom's stupid play.

DAX

I didn't beg. I just asked.

JOSH

No way. You begged.

(This exchange makes them both a little uncomfortable. Rather than sit still and stare at the floor, Josh scoots off the table he's been perched on. Not to be outdone, Dax stands up. They essentially trade places, but are ultra-careful not to even brush each other as they pass.)

DAX

(after a couple of beats) I think Cooper did what he said.

JOSH

Cooper's sixteen, and he's all of a sudden your best friend?

DAX

He told me about Amber.

JOSH

Just you?

DAX

And some other guys.

JOSH

So you were on the fringe.

DAX

It didn't sound like a lie. He knew stuff.

JOSH

You can make stuff up.

DAX

He's had a lot of girlfriends.

JOSH

He *says* he's had a lot of girlfriends.

DAX

He's got a car. When you've got a car, you've got girlfriends.

JOSH

What you've got is passengers.

(Dax thinks this over as Josh flips through his script.)

JOSH

What's this play supposed to be about, anyway?

DAX

Mom says it's a penetrating indictment of corporate greed.

(There's a small commotion offstage, followed by the sound of a slammed door. Carol enters, looking exasperated. She glances at the boys, but she's really talking to herself.)

CAROL

He's supposed to be the Prince of Darkness. Well, the Prince of Darkness can't prance. He has to stride. Who do I call to get a new Prince of Darkness? *(staring at her cell phone)*

JOSH

(whispers) Who's she talking about?

DAX

(whispers) Angelica Dorfman's dad. God, if she gets rid of him, Angelica won't show up; and if Angelica doesn't show up, I got both of us into this for nothing.

(Carol closes her cell with a decisive snap and turns to her son and Josh.)

CAROL
(sharply) Are you boys ready? Do you know your lines?

JOSH
Yes, ma'am.

DAX
Yes, Mom.
(Carol exits. The boys look at each other.)

DAX
Sometimes she makes me go want to live in a cave.

JOSH
Which wouldn't be so bad if Angelica Dorfman was there, right?

DAX
And the cave had cable.

JOSH
So I'm not playing basketball right now because you think Angelica's going to find you irresistible in these cardboard wings.

DAX

You know Angelica, man. Talk about inordinately fair limbs.

JOSH

Check this out. *(Josh opens the book he has been holding. He searches for a particular page.)* A guy in here writes his name all over his girlfriend's body.

DAX

Everywhere?

JOSH

I wonder if people really do stuff like that or is it all made up?

DAX

Sure, they do.

JOSH

(tapping the book cover) And then she gets a tattoo.

DAX

Angelica would never get a tattoo. Amber's got one, though. Cooper said so.

JOSH

Dax, kids can't get tattoos. You have to be eighteen.

DAX

Hers is probably someplace nobody can see it.

JOSH

The guy who did it would see it. He's the one
who'd get in trouble.

DAX

She looks eighteen sometimes.

JOSH

Doesn't matter. It says right on the window of that
place uptown: WE CHECK ID.

DAX

You can get fake IDs anywhere.

JOSH

For instance?

DAX

The bad part of town.

JOSH

Like you go there a lot.

DAX

Screw you, Joshua. Do you even know Amber
Franklin?

JOSH

She goes to King.

DAX

A lot of girls go to King.

JOSH

I know who she is.

DAX

Would *you* do it to her if you could?

JOSH

(*after a beat*) It's always that way, isn't it?

DAX

What way?

JOSH

Would you do it to her. Why not, "Would you do it *with* her?"

DAX

Okay. Would you do it *with* her?

JOSH

I don't know. Would you do it with Angelica Dorfman?

DAX

Are you kidding? I've only talked to her twice.
Really talked, I mean. *(after a beat or two)* Cooper
says Amber likes him because he's lanky.

JOSH

Lanky boys with cars.

DAX

I'm kind of lanky.

JOSH

Get serious. Angelica's like a foot taller than you.

DAX

(frowning) Cooper says *he* does it to Amber on a
tofu.

JOSH

Tofu?

DAX

Futon. What'd I say?

JOSH

Tofu.

DAX

I meant futon.

JOSH

Now it's just another sordid tale.

DAX

You say the weirdest things. Is that why you
wouldn't do it to Amber? Because it'd be sordid?

JOSH

(adjusting his wings, which make it hard to sit back
comfortably) I think it might be.

DAX

With anybody or just with Amber?

JOSH

I don't know.

DAX

Your dad gets Showtime, doesn't he?

JOSH

Yeah.

DAX

That can be sordid.

JOSH

I wouldn't want it to be like Showtime.

DAX

Cooper says Amber is such a slut.

JOSH

See, there's that.

DAX

There's what?

JOSH

Calling people names. He does sordid things and then calls the other person names.

DAX

Cooper says the futon is in his garage.

JOSH

That's romantic: "Just lie down by the lawn mower, darling."

DAX

Yeah. Between the Weedwacker and my old bike.

JOSH

Sounds like you've been there.

DAX

In his garage? Yeah.

JOSH

Was there a futon?

DAX

No, but he could drag it out from the house.

JOSH

And his mother wouldn't see?

DAX

His mother works.

JOSH

Like that interferes with her omniscience.
(Dax looks baffled.)

It means they know everything. Moms, I mean.

DAX

I suppose you can spell it, too.

JOSH

O-M-N-I—

DAX

(interrupting) My father gave me a condom.

JOSH

No way.

DAX

He said, "Do you know what this is?" I said, "Yes."
He said, "Don't be stupid."

JOSH

Have you still got it?

DAX

I sort of experimented.

JOSH

Just in case?

DAX

Exactly. And it takes some time.

JOSH

Yeah?

DAX

What's the girl supposed to do while you, you
know, get ready?

JOSH

Bring a book, maybe. Promote literacy.
(*Carol peeks around a corner.*)

CAROL

Boys?

DAX

Yeah, Mom.

JOSH

Yes, ma'am.

CAROL

(She enters.) I've got Mr. Dorfman all calmed down, so when you hear the music, that's your cue. Count three, and come onstage. (She inspects them, then smiles.) You look nice. (She exits.)

DAX

(after a beat or two) My mom looks at me sometimes and says junk like, "Oh, honey. I hate for you to grow up."

JOSH

I don't care how lanky he is or how many cars he's got, no way is Cooper Anderson grown up.

DAX

Have you made out with a girl?

JOSH

At parties.

DAX

I wonder how you get from there to the other?

JOSH

The other?

DAX

What my dad gave me the condom for. I can't imagine me and that thing and Angelica.

JOSH

Maybe Cooper Anderson knows.

DAX

He'd probably just lie some more.
(*Carol's head appears again.*)

CAROL

Boys? Get ready.

JOSH

How do I look?

DAX

Stupid.
(*Dax adjusts Josh's wings.*)

JOSH

What do we do when we get out there?

DAX

Combat the forces of darkness.

JOSH

So we have to fight Angelica Dorfman's dad?

DAX

Mom said to just dazzle him with our purity.

JOSH

(thoughtfully) I don't think I feel as pure as I used to.

DAX

Look—when we're done, let's take off these wings and shoot some hoops.

JOSH

At my house, okay? It's closer to Angelica Dorfman's, and it's farther away from Cooper Anderson's.

DAX

That guy. He's the Prince of Darkness if you ask me.

JOSH

Nah. He's just some stupid kid.

DAX

(after a beat) He *is* stupid, isn't he.

JOSH

Totally.
(Music from offstage. The boys count one, two, three and exit, not one after the other but side by side.)

BUCKING

BALES

BY Raymond Bial

Early one summer, my father came home and announced, "I quit my job."

Glancing up anxiously from the kitchen sink, Mom asked, "Why would you go and quit your job?"

"We're moving!" my father said. "Back to Illinois."

"What for?" Mom asked.

"I'm homesick," my father groaned, as though he had a bellyache.

Folding her arms, my mother declared, "Well, I'm not moving. I like it here, and so do the kids."

No one in the family, except my father, wanted to move "back home," as he called it. However, my father insisted, "I'm the man of the house! And we're moving back home!"

We had already moved five times in my young life,

but I had come to especially love this farm and could not imagine leaving it. Mom insisted that she was not going to move again. There were arguments.

I was now thirteen and felt it was time for me to get a job, to become more independent. Each evening, I measured the height and width of my shadow on the side of our white house, just before sunset. My voice had deepened, and I had gotten my growth, having shot up to five-foot-ten. I was also eating as much as I could to put weight on my slender frame.

I wanted to bale hay, which was the most readily available summer job for country boys. Bucking bales was also an excellent way to get in shape for football, which had recently become another dream of mine. Of course, not many farmers were hiring skinny thirteen-year-olds to buck bales of hay and straw. I doubted whether I could get a job that summer.

Then one day my mom heard about a baling job with a local farmer. "It pays a dollar an hour," she said. "It's yours if you want it."

I imagined myself working heroically bucking bales, getting stronger by the moment, earning my own money, and readily agreed to do so.

Farmers usually started baling hay after the dew had

dried on the windrows—in late morning or afternoon. The next day I did chores and hoed in my vegetable garden until just before noon. I then got my beat-up straw cowboy hat and a pair of leather gloves off the shelf on the back porch. I could drive every vehicle on our farm—car, truck, tractor, and jeep—but wasn't old enough for a license. So Mom drove me in the pickup, down the lane and along the county roads. Putting a sober expression on my face, I stared ahead as the pickup, faded to a powder blue, swayed with the blacktop, as if on the high seas.

I was almost lulled to sleep by the air blustering through the windows and the rocking motion of the pickup when Mom turned off the highway and we banged up a long farm lane bordered by a row of hedge-apple trees.

I sat up in the bench seat and squinted at the T-shaped farmhouse, barn, outbuildings, and feedlot as she turned around in the backyard.

"You call when you're through baling for the day," she said. "I'll pick you up."

"Thanks," I muttered. My mother had always been the salvation of my brothers, sister, and myself. Hardworking and cheerful, she encouraged us to better ourselves—and made us believe that we could. She was the opposite of our father, who never had a good word for anyone.

I climbed out of the pickup and raised my hand to wave good-bye as she pulled back down the drive. I walked up to the back porch of the house and knocked on the screen door.

A woman in her midforties appeared in the doorway. She squinted into the bright noon sun. "Yes?"

I swallowed. "I've come to work…uh…baling hay."

Her eyes narrowing, the woman appeared disappointed. She stood there a moment, as though at a loss. She had swirls of gray in her hair like marble cake and thin lines about her eyes.

I told her, "I'm on the light side, but I can do the work."

She sighed. "I'll have to ask my husband. We're still at dinner, but he'll be out shortly."

I stood there, not sure if I had a job or not—or if I even wanted it now.

"You can wait under that oak tree," she said. "It's nice and shady there."

I was about to thank her when she dissolved back into the gray interior of the house.

As I strolled to the shade tree, the sweat was already trickling down my back, yet I was determined to prove myself on this job. A few minutes later, the screen door slammed, and I whirled around to face a lean man in a chambray shirt and faded jeans, striding toward me.

I was instantly short of breath.

Thrusting out a thick hand, the man boomed, "I'm Harry Proctor!"

I accepted the hand, but my throat was so knotted up that I could only nod an acknowledgment.

"You got a name?" the man asked.

"Uh...Ray."

Harry Proctor grunted, "I'll try you on the wagon."

My stomach tightened.

We walked across the yard. He swung into the seat of a Farmall tractor, and I clambered up beside him. Half standing on the axle, half sitting on the fender, I rode with him around the backyard and down the winding lane.

Pulling off his seed-corn cap, Harry wiped his forearm across his brow and said, "It's going to be a scorcher. Paper said it might hit a hundred today."

Setting my jaw, I lied. "I don't mind."

Harry snorted as though he could see right through me. "Well, you're sure going to get a bellyful today."

The sun had arced overhead. There was not a hint of a cloud, and the hedge-apple trees stood so still that I wondered if they would ever move again. We turned into a field wrapped with rolling windrows of freshly raked hay. I hopped down and hitched the baler to the tractor and a wagon to the baler with large bolts that felt cool in the palms of my hands.

"You've got gloves, don't you?" Harry yelled back as I scrambled onto the wagon.

I waved my gloves.

"They cowhide?"

"Yeah."

Twisting around in the seat, Harry propped his foot on the fender. "Once had a boy come to work for me with cloth gloves. Wasn't two hours and those gloves were in shreds." He revved the tractor. "Come to think of it, that boy didn't last too long himself!"

Yet I knew about gloves. I also wore a cowboy hat for protection against the blistering sun and my old tennis shoes for surer footing on the wagon.

"On a day like this you can get heatstroke in no time

flat," the man shouted cheerfully as he eased the procession forward—tractor, baler, and wagon—until he was lined up with the outside windrow.

I braced myself on the wagon.

When the first bale pounded up the chute, I stabbed it with the hay hook, lugged it to the back of the wagon, and stacked it against the hayrack.

After that, the bales came like clockwork, always just ahead of me, and I hustled to keep up with them. No sooner had I stacked one bale than another was tipping off the chute, and I rushed to the front of the wagon to catch it. Wire-tied, they weighed sixty to seventy pounds each—more than half as much as I, but I gritted my teeth and kept baling.

About a half hour later, I had loaded the wagon—four bales high with a row of bales called a tie-string across the top. We left it by the gate, hitched the next wagon to the baler, and simply repeated the process. Another hand, driving an old Farmall tractor, picked up the loaded wagon and drove it back to the barn.

In the brief moments between bales I quickly stripped off my T-shirt and hooked it on a corner of the hayrack, where it hung like a limp, white flag in the shimmering heat.

Occasionally, Harry twisted around to survey our progress, but the rackety baler was too loud to shout over. So he had to rely upon a wave or a smile. Chaff sticking to my sweaty chest, short of breath, I daydreamed myself into oblivion as I loaded wagon after wagon.

Even with gloves, a row of blisters was rising on my palms. From my fingertips to my shoulders the muscles had knotted, and by the fourth wagonload—or was it the fifth?—my legs were getting heavy on me. As the afternoon progressed, I struggled to keep up with the baler. It became harder for me to stack the high, fourth tier of bales that had to be shoved over my head.

Around four o'clock, judging by the sun, the woman I had met at the back door drove into the field in a dust-lightened Willys jeep. Stopping the tractors, the man disengaged the baler and shut off the engine.

I sagged down on a bale atop the load of hay.

Pivoting around in the tractor seat, Harry Proctor extended a gallon jug toward me. "Drink?"

I scrambled down to the tractor. I had likely sweated away several of my slender 135 pounds.

Tilting the jug over his knee, Harry filled a tin cup and handed it to me.

Wordlessly, I gulped the lukewarm water. Seconds later, I was holding out the cup for more.

Harry chuckled. "Handiest thing I carry on this tractor."

The woman, whom he'd called Opal, waited until I had gotten a second cupful before she announced, her words thinned by the open space, "Those two boys you hired this morning, they up and quit. Said it was too hot."

Harry banged his fist on the upper lip of the steering wheel. "Dang, if that don't leave us in one heck of a fix."

He studied the remaining windrows for a moment, then said to Opal, "You might help Mike set up for milking once he gets done pulling the wagons back to the barn. But we'll make out all right. Just don't expect us in too early." He nodded to me as I was gulping my fourth cupful of water. "This boy's one hard worker, I'll say that for him."

Harry had made the remark offhandedly, but I was thrilled.

We worked through the bulk of that hot afternoon and late into the evening. The intense, yellow globe of sun descended in the sky, to the edge of the distant fields. Shadows lengthened and the day gradually lost its color. When we traced the last windrow, the sun was obscured behind the ragged line of trees, and the air had become gray and lightless.

Every muscle and every joint in my body ached. My fingers had stiffened inside the sweaty gloves, and the insides of my arms were crisscrossed with scratches from hay stems. In the cooling air, the sweat had dried on my torso, which was caked with chaff, but my jeans were still ringing wet.

I longed to flop into bed—although, come to think of it, I still had chores ahead of me at home—when Harry braked the tractor, nearly toppling me off the wagon.

"What the heck," I muttered.

Without a word, Harry pointed to a dozen or so bales, which had fallen from the back corner of the wagon. Releasing a weary sigh, I jumped down and hurriedly wedged the bales back into place. I flinched when the man approached me in long, resolute strides. Expecting him to holler at me, even raise his fist, as my own father would have done, I backed away. However, he casually snatched up a bale and whizzed it onto the top of the load. "You're getting a pretty good workout today," he roared, smiling so broadly that his teeth gleamed in the dusk.

I stared at him. "It's not so bad."

Harry snorted. "I'm nearly shot myself and I just drove the tractor. You've done yourself proud, son."

"I'm getting in shape for football," I blurted.

"Football!" Harry bellowed. "If you can work at the game like you worked for me today, you're going to make one heck of a football player!"

Within myself, I was aglow. My own father had always been so mean and critical, and here was this stranger heaping praise upon me.

After reloading the bales, we drove back down the highway, in the thickening dusk. In contrast to the heat of the day, the breeze was cool and sent shivers through me.

Parking the tractor in the yard, we headed to the barn, where the regular hand, Mike, was already milking. Harry casually asked me, "You want to work tomorrow?"

"Yes!" I answered, delighted that I had proven myself in his eyes.

"If you want to wait until we at least get started here, I'll give you a ride home."

My lips dry, barely able to keep my eyes open, I told him, "Thanks."

Over the next few days, I worked late into each evening for Harry Proctor, after which he drove me home. The blisters on my palms quickly hardened into calluses, the muscles tightened across my shoulders, and my torso browned more deeply. Carefully, from a distance, I came to like Harry. He was a strong man of light colors—gray eyes, faded jeans, and thinning hair—his forehead white across the top, where it was covered by the seed-corn cap. Harry worked with the spring of a young man. Unlike my father, he was always in a cheerful mood.

Since we were busy in the fields every day, Harry and I didn't have much time for talk. But I had already heard enough lectures from my father to last me several lifetimes, and I appreciated Harry for his unspoken example.

Thursday evening, when all the alfalfa was baled and stacked in the barn, Harry and I drove back to the house, the sun making long shadows of us. Usually, as soon as we returned from the fields, Harry drove me home, saying, "You've put in a good day. Get yourself some rest." But that night as we chugged back to the house with the last load of hay he asked, "You want to help with the milking?"

"Sure!"

Harry chuckled. "You're one easygoing guy. I swear you love to work!"

"I do," I said.

As we walked into the blaze of lights in the milking parlor, Mike was ushering the first set of cows into stanchions. He had slicked-back hair like James Dean and a tattoo of a heart on his right arm, just below a pack of Pall Mall cigarettes rolled into his T-shirt sleeve.

"How's it going here?" boomed Harry.

"Pretty good."

Harry sighed. "We're awful late with the milking again tonight. We're going to have to start keeping more regular hours, aren't we, Ray?"

I smiled. "That'd be all right with me." I noticed that creamy yellow milk was streaming from the full udder of one large Holstein cow.

"We'll be done in no time flat with you guys helping," Mike said as he clamped portable milking machines on the first three cows' udders and proceeded to milk the fourth cow by hand.

Harry asked me, "Ever milked?"

"Some."

"Want to give it a whirl?"

I shrugged. "Sure."

Next thing I knew I was seated beside a stately Holstein cow, the black-and-white map on her flank directly in my face. I squeezed the teats and the milk rang into the stainless-steel bucket, but the rising foam soon muffled the sound.

The serene atmosphere in the barn reminded me of the Nativity. It felt good to work among the gentle animals, in a place where I felt comfortable, for a while. After the long day's work, as the milk hissed in the buckets, I was unable to suppress a yawn.

"You must be dead on your feet," remarked Harry.

"I'm all right."

Harry laughed. "I bet you'd say that if you were about to drop in your tracks."

I merely shrugged.

"Lemme give you a hand."

As Harry replaced me on the three-legged stool and briskly stripped the cow's udder, he remarked, "You two boys have sure done yourselves proud this week."

Mike and I exchanged glances of quiet pride.

As we finished the milking and Mike began to hose down the concrete floor, Harry asked, "You go to high school in Edwardsburg, Ray?"

"Shoot, no!" I grinned and looked at my shuffling feet. "I just finished seventh grade."

Harry scratched his head. "Just how old are you, son?"

"Thirteen."

"Thirteen!"

Grinning, Mike said, "They're sure growing 'em big these days."

Harry yanked off his cap and swatted his thigh. "I'll be danged! And here I've been working your tail off all week! Those two boys who quit the other day were eighteen and nineteen, and you done better'n them by a mile! I'd have figured you for sixteen at least."

I couldn't keep the grin off my face. Nobody had ever taken this much interest in me.

My ears burning, I swallowed and explained, "I'll turn fourteen in November. That's not so far off."

"I never!" Harry shook his head repeatedly.

*　*　*

All that week I immersed myself in Harry Proctor's place, which I came to love as much as my own little farm. Harry couldn't seem to get over my being so young, and he praised my work more than ever. I was also proud that Harry had not hired other hands to replace the guys who had quit the first day, since he could rely on Mike and me to bring in the hay.

The pay was a dollar an hour. On Saturday evening, Harry handed me a check for fifty-six dollars, the amount matching the number of hours I had worked in the six days of that week.

I smiled as I folded the salmon-colored check and slipped it into a corner of my wallet. I couldn't wait to get home to show Mom this solid proof of my worth.

Harry then explained: "Come Monday, I'm hoping the dew will be dry on the hay early so we can start baling midmorning, You can have dinner with us, if you like."

I had never been invited to anyone's house before and considered it a great honor—and a cause for anxiety, since I'd never been much of a talker. All Monday morning, as I worked on the wagon, I wondered what I might say at dinner. But as it turned out, Harry did enough talking for everyone.

As Opal placed bowls of steaming boiled potatoes, green beans fresh from the garden, and a platter of roast beef on the table, Harry practically told me his life story. "Got a boy myself—he's in the army." I also found out that Harry had been farming all his life. He grew up in Nebraska, then moved to Opal's family farm in southern Michigan when they got married. "It's a lot tougher now," he said. "But we're making it, aren't we, Opal?"

So, this was how families sat down to meals, I thought, with pleasant conversation and good food. At home, the best that we could expect was that my father would only brood and not lose his temper altogether.

Thereafter, Harry invited me to have lunch with them several times a week, whenever it was dry enough to start baling early. Friday afternoon, Harry told me, "When we're done with the first cutting of the hay, I'll find other work for you until the hay grows back and it's time for second and third cutting. Also got straw to bale—from our winter wheat crop. There are plenty of jobs that need doing around here, Ray. That is, if you want to keep working steady."

"Oh, I want to work!" I told him.

Harry declared to Opal, "There's not a job Ray won't take on."

I grinned broadly.

"Heck, you'd muck out cow stalls if I asked you to, wouldn't you?"

"Sure!"

I wondered if Harry was going out of his way to find work for me because he liked having me around, perhaps because he missed his own children, who had grown and left the farm, especially his son in the army.

I had begun this job as a means of proving myself and gaining some independence. But now, more importantly, I was working among people who appreciated me, and I was beginning to feel part of Harry's family.

The next evening, Harry and I got back late from baling hay. Meeting us in the yard, Opal said, "Cows must have drifted to the hedgerow."

Usually, the cows gathered in the feedlot at milking time, but apparently they'd gotten tired of waiting for us. Getting chalk on his elbows, Harry leaned against the whitewashed fence rail overlooking the pasture. Cupping his hands around his mouth, Harry called melodiously, somewhere between a song and a plain holler. We gazed out across the field, where Queen Anne's lace bobbed in the wind.

The string of cows loped over the rise, dust at their heels, silhouetted against the evening sky.

Opal chuckled. "He can make them come in any speed. The faster he calls, the faster they come into the lot."

Harry increased the cadence of his call, and the cows broke into a trot. When he slowed the rhythm of his voice, they slipped back into a walk. Just for the heck of it, he brought the cows into the feedlot at a dead run.

"That's amazing," I said.

Harry chuckled. "There's not much to it. The cows pretty much teach themselves. Whenever I introduce a new cow to the herd, she just learns from the others."

It was pretty near magic, I thought. I decided that I wanted to become a farmer, just like Harry.

Day after day, I worked for Harry Proctor. With the air carrying the fragrance of alfalfa, freshly cut, I was surprised at how quickly the summer was passing—we were already starting the third cutting of hay. Studying me closely, Harry asked, "I don't mean to pry, but I saw a 'For Sale' sign at your farm. You folks moving?"

I was stunned. "Well, my…uh…dad wants to move back to Illinois, but…"

"Illinois?" asked Harry.

I shrugged. "My dad says he's homesick. But I'm not sure if we're really going."

Soon after, everyone in the family, except me, drove about two hundred miles southwest to my parents' hometown of Danville, Illinois, to look for a house. I was left behind to take care of our livestock. I was happy to stay home.

"Don't worry," Mom assured me. "He can move, but I'm staying here. I'm just going to visit your grandfather."

Each morning for the next three days, while alone on the farm, I did chores and then went to work on Harry Proctor's farm. In the evenings at home, I ran my heart out, dodging trees and jumping logs in the woods, to get in shape for football. I blazed across the fields until I was exhausted, and then I pushed myself harder, reaching beyond myself, into the thin air before me.

On Sunday afternoon, everyone came home, my brothers and sisters whooping, "We bought a new house!" I searched my mother's eyes. Finally, she explained, "Your grandfather is getting up in years.

It might not be a bad idea to be around home again."

"But I want to stay here. I thought—" I cut myself off. What was the use? I was too young to be on my own. I would have to move with them. I tore down the slope to be alone in the bottom ground. I walked along the creek, thinking of the land I'd grown to love so deeply—and of Harry and Opal. I couldn't imagine moving away. I would miss them so badly. I might never see them again. Why had I ever gone to work on their farm? If I had stayed home and kept to myself, I wouldn't be hurting, at least not this much.

The days went by as if in a dream. My father sold our farm, and we were suddenly about to move away. It came to the last day that I would ever work for Harry Proctor. Toward evening, the man backed the last load of hay into the barn.

"Want to give me a hand with this load?" he asked.

I shinnied up the board ladder to the loft while Harry climbed atop the load of hay.

"Ready?"

"Anytime."

Bale after bale charged over the beam and tumbled onto the loft floor. I hauled them to the wall and stacked them to the rafters. The hard, steady work soothed and satisfied me. If only my life could be this simple and myself this able.

Halfway through the load, Harry gritted his teeth and asked, "Getting tired?"

I kicked another bale into place. "No way."

As we worked through the load, I thought about the time I had put in at the Proctor farm. In this brief season, I was just a hired hand; I was just passing through. I didn't mean that much to these people, not as much as they meant to me. And then, just like that, we were finished unloading the hay.

Harry swung down from the wagon and shook the chaff from his flannel shirt. That was when I told him, "I guess we're moving after all."

Harry stopped cold. "Back home?"

"In the morning."

I thought I saw a torn look in Harry's eyes. However, sticking out his hand, he said with good humor, "Don't that beat all? Best of luck to you, son."

I accepted the hand, the first time we had shaken hands since the day I started to work on this farm.

"It's been good having you here," said Harry.

I was on the verge of tears.

He sighed. "We'd better settle up. I believe I owe you a week's pay."

As far as I was concerned, this man had already paid me much more than enough, the memory of which I would carry with me for the rest of my life.

I hoped that Harry would call to me as I left, saying, "Hey, I need a regular hand. You want to work year-round?"

The next day we climbed into the car and drove away. We moved to a small farm north of Danville, but I never felt much for the new place.

All I had left of my dreams was the chance to play football—that way I imagined Harry and Opal would be proud of me. I had put on fifteen pounds of muscle that summer and weighed 150 pounds when I played football in eighth grade. I had a fine coach, who once nodded toward me and said casually to a teammate, "Ray is going to be one heck of a football player."

I sometimes imagined Harry coming to watch me at the games. I always competed with a singular, burning anger at what had been taken away from me.

Over the years, I often thought about getting in

touch with Harry and Opal—but it always seemed so distant and impossible. Yet I never forgot them. More than thirty years after my summer of bucking bales, I finally picked up the phone and called, talking with Opal, then Harry. Thereafter, we occasionally talked on the phone and exchanged brief notes. Then, one summer day, a car pulled into our driveway. I did not recognize the old couple at first—but it was Harry and Opal. They were just passing through, on their way to visit Harry's family in Nebraska, and decided to stop by. To see them again after all these years was one of the greatest thrills of my life. Curiously, that same week, I had been photographing young men bucking bales on a family farm and thinking of those long-ago days when I stood tall on a hay wagon, riding the high seas of the American heartland.

THE TEN-TON ACCORDION

BY Barry Kornhauser

You want to play *what?*"

"You heard me, Pop."

My father, like so many parents who had grown up in the Great Depression, wanted his kids to have all the things my mother and he had missed out on—whether we wanted them or not. Music lessons neared the top of that list. *My* own list of wants was slightly different, the foremost being: (1) pet monkey, (2) suit of armor, (3) stuffed moose head, (4) genuine Civil War sword, and (5) ride in a deep-sea bathysphere. A band instrument with accompanying instruction didn't even make it onto the top one hundred. But when I saw there was no changing my parents' minds, I decided to embrace the notion and, after careful deliberation, announced that I had opted to study and master…the accordion.

I could see in the furtive glances shot back and forth between the folks that the humble squeeze box wasn't exactly what they had in mind. While ironing our underwear, Mom would listen devotedly to the stuffiest of stations on our radio, dreaming that her firstborn son would one day join the ranks of those classical musicians she adored whose names were as foreign-sounding as any in our neighborhood. And here I was, brazenly flushing those dreams right down the drain, my father's hard-earned money swirling right behind.

"Why not the clarinet?" appealed the old man. He bore a striking resemblance to Benny Goodman, a fellow pictured tooting the skinny black woodwind on record jackets piled high near our hi-fi.

"Or the French horn!" piped in Mom, who, for reasons never understood by anyone in the family, admired everything *français*, even though the closest she ever came to France was making French toast for breakfast and seeing the movie *Gigi* five times.

Music lessons represented only the latest front in the ongoing Berwick Street Culture War. This was my folks' valiant campaign to win their children's hearts and minds over to the arts and other lofty pursuits, a lost cause if ever there was one. Every August we were dragged kicking and screaming to see "Shakespeare in the Park." But Shakespeare in Warinanco Park was not exactly the stuff dreams are made on. My baby brother, Lee, blissfully slept through it all. But middle brother David and I spent at least one act squirming in our seats beneath our parents' threatening glares and "shushes" loud enough to drown out the very lines that were supposed to uplift us. Salvation usually came about midway through Act II, when the folks would inevitably join little Lee in the land of Nod, and David and I could spend the remainder of the evening hanging upside down under the bleacher seats, trying to see who could last the longest before passing out.

Nor were the other arts ignored. Back home, presumably hanging right-side up on every available spot of wall, was the complete collection of our Uncle Al's oil paintings. These were true modern masterpieces...of the *color-by-number* variety. My mistaken notion arising from this work, that there was a direct connection between canvas and math, kept me from ever thinking to raise a paintbrush myself. Dance we were thankfully spared altogether. We were *boys*, after all, and even my mother knew better than to attempt so much as a single sugarplum fairy or dying swan. Visits to local museums usually ended in groundings after Dave and I invariably forgot the "Please Don't Touch" rule and tried to shove dead staghorn-beetle specimens down each other's pants or convince little Lee to use every colonial-era powder horn as a bugle.

Which brings me back to music. And the accordion. I had put a lot of thought into this choice of instrument. In our neighborhood, the true sign of emerging status was having an upright piano in the living room. The DeTulas got an upright not long after Mr. D began driving his own ice-cream truck, and he was more proud of that piano than he was of the business that had made its purchase possible. His usual frosty demeanor would melt quicker than an Eskimo Pie in July every time one of the little DeTulas pecked out the tune of his truck's jingle on its ivories. I realized that a piano was out of the question for us if only because, with four generations residing in the same household, space was at a premium. As it was, my great-grandmother's foldout bed took up much of the living room. But I had a better idea anyway. Wasn't the accordion—with its cleverly condensed keyboard—just like a portable piano? One you could take with you to *any* room of the house or, for that matter, anywhere else—be it corner drugstore or White Castle burger joint ?

Clearly impressed by this logic, my father came home not long after with a large blue suitcase. "Open it," he said, beaming, as my mother, hands still dripping dishwashing liquid, looked on. I hesitated, my thumb gently stroking the knob of the first brass latch. "Go on! Go on!" encouraged the old man.

"Wait! Wait!" shouted Mom. "Get in here, everybody! Quick! It's here!"

Brothers, grandmother, and great-grandmother descended upon the scene and even a few neighbors, including Mr. and Mrs. Klingenthal from across the street, who had been invited to shoot this historic moment with their eight-millimeter movie camera. *Here goes nothing,* I thought. A quick press on the knob, and—*snap!*—the first latch popped open, followed by burbles of approval. I took a deep breath and pressed again. *Snap!* Up flew the second! More congratulatory murmurs. Slowly now, very slowly, I raised the lid, half expecting another of my old man's cheesy practical jokes, like that can of peanut brittle that, when opened,

sent fabric snakes rocketing toward anything break-
able. What I found instead was the bulk of the suitcase's contents protectively draped by a velvety cloth
the same deep blue color as the night sky over the
nearby Linden refineries. I swallowed, closed my eyes,
and ever so tenderly drew back this mantle. A hush
descended upon the room. I opened my eyes. One at a
time. Beneath that veil was the most beautiful thing I
had ever seen in my life, with the possible exception of
Rhonda Castilfidardo and the cover of Adventure Comic
#247.

An accordion. My accordion! It was as white as Mr.
D's vanilla ice cream, with inlaid mother-of-pearl
accents and fire-engine-red trim. One of its buttons had
what appeared to be an actual diamond set in its center. And the adjustable straps looked exactly like the
kind of leather gear you'd see hooked up to a horse in
the Westerns shown at the Elmora movie theater
around the corner. This wasn't just an instrument; it
was an invitation to adventure!

"It's not new," noted the old man, "but you wouldn't
know it. It was only played on Sundays by a little-old-
lady polka band."

"Give it a squeeze!" cried Mom, playfully swatting

Pop and sprinkling the living room with little bubbles of Joy.

I bent over to raise the treasure from its secure blue vault, and right then and there, although I didn't realize it at the time, I experienced the beginning of the end of my life in music. As hard as I tried, I couldn't budge the accordion; it was too heavy for me to lift! I was small for my age and underweight, the result of having been born premature. My birth, joked the old man, was the only time in my life I was "early for anything." Mostly I didn't mind my size—or lack of it. While Rhonda Castilfidardo might have overlooked me, so did most of the neighborhood bullies, who probably figured I wasn't much of a catch. Even at Warinanco Lake, you threw the little fish back. I would take some sort of crooked pride in consistently fooling the Guess Your Age booth operators at local fairs, and I could win any hide-and-seek game by packing myself into anything not much larger than our Plymouth's glove compartment. Part of my very reason for choosing this instrument was that, like me, it seemed an abridged version of a full-size model. We seemed made for each other. Leave the piano for those whose toes could reach the pedals. My fingers would caress the diamond-encrusted button of my squeeze box. Only now I couldn't pick the thing up!

Feeling just a little betrayed, I plopped down on the sofa as my old man got the accordion out of its case and sat it on my lap. I swung my arms into those cowhide straps, and Mom began to adjust them—or tried to. Even at their tightest setting, they were way too big for me. When I leaned forward in an attempt to better bear its weight, the accordion straps dropped off my shoulders and the instrument slipped out of my hands like one of those Warinanco fish, slick with natural oils and petroleum products. I don't know what made a more terrible sound—the accordion as it flopped onto the floor or my horrified parents' screams.

While the instrument was rescued by my father and fussily checked for damage, Mom headed back into the kitchen, having been struck by an idea. She returned moments later with a still-damp dish towel, which she looped between the two straps behind my back and tied with a granny knot. Now, securely fastened to the accordion by my mother's clever device, I confidently leaned forward once more. Big mistake. Like *Moby Dick's* Captain Ahab, caught in his harpoon line, I was attached to my own white whale. This time, as the instrument dove for the floor, it took me with it!

Now it was my pop's turn to be brilliant. "Flo," he said to my mom, who was Florence to everyone else, "get me a couple more dish towels!"

By the time she returned with the goods, I had been picked up off the carpet by the old man and propped into an old wooden chair. No time to check me for damages; his idea was ready to be tested. Not only was I to be fastened to the accordion, but now also to the chair itself. The extra dish towels, tied together in a chain around the straps, bound me *and* the accordion to the back of the seat. To everyone's surprise—Pop's included—the plan worked. Like a charm. There was no way I would ever again fall down on my beautiful new used instrument.

Unfortunately, there was also no way I could get up. I was its prisoner until someone freed me. Naively, I did not foresee this as a problem. As I couldn't begin practicing until someone rigged me up, I assumed quite naturally that there would always be someone there to engineer my release one half hour later. I was now ready to bring song into the world. Only, as I was soon to find out, the world wasn't ready for me.

There's a classic old joke about one of New York City's most famous concert stages. One man stops another on the street and asks: "How do you get to Carnegie Hall?" The other guy replies: "Practice!" Somehow I don't think this notion applies to tone-deaf eight-year-olds with accordions. For a while I thought things were going along quite smoothly, that my parents found "Carnival of Venice" a pleasant enough tune to bear repeated listening. Much repeated listening. Then one day the old man had "an inspiration!" Since the weather was so nice, wouldn't I prefer to practice on the screened-in front porch?

The next thing I knew I was tied to an accordion and a chair just outside the front door—the *closed* front door. But that was okay. The weather *was* nice, and the "carnival" of music seemed to fit the hustle and bustle of the block. Sometimes I'd get a little wistful watching the guys play punchball in the street, and would holler "Car!" for them, being able to spot the vehicular intruder from my elevated vantage point well before they could. I'll admit I had a hard time concentrating when they'd play "Bike Chicken," a sport we invented in 1959. Competitors would crash their bicycles into one another as fast and hard as possible (an early "Extreme Sport" that somehow never caught on beyond a two-block radius).

On occasion, the dreaded Charlie "the Hose" Trossingen would saunter by, his water gun primed and readied as always. Seeing me captive on my porch, he'd fire away through the screen, soaking my sheet music and me before running off, cackling madly, to drown his next unsuspecting victim. (Trossingen continued to plague everyone this way for a few more years, until his day of reckoning arrived via an unintended squirting episode so terrible that it immortalized him in the pages of neighborhood history, cemented his infamy, and taught me the meaning of divine justice. One afternoon during social studies, our neighborhood menace found himself suddenly overcome by flu. Clamping his hand tightly over his mouth in a desperate attempt to avert the inevitable, Charlie "the Hose" projectile-vomited the length of the entire classroom... through his nose!)

Still, all in all, the front porch was a pretty good gig. Sometimes I can't help but think that all might have ended quite differently had the next-door neighbors on both sides not felt the same about their own front porches, from which they would enjoy a summer breeze, some local gossip, and the occasional Bike Chicken match. In fact, about the only thing in the world they *didn't* seem to enjoy from those front porches of theirs was "Carnival of Venice."

So I next found myself banished to the *back* porch. But that didn't last long either. Mrs. House-on-the-Left complained that my "noise"—"NOISE?"—was keeping her baby from napping. When my folks moved me into the middle of our backyard, Mr. House-on-the-Right grumbled that my playing was stunting the growth of the squashes in his vegetable patch. Eventually, my accordion, dish towels, and chair were shunted off, far away from all humanity, to a patch of crabgrass at the very rear of our yard. This bordered a small neglected area between streets that the gang called "the Woods," not for its single scraggly tree, but because it was the main habitat of the area's native wildlife—squirrels, a possum or two, and an ever-expanding pack of touchy stray cats.

That I might catch rabies from any of these creatures was one of the three great fears of my childhood (the others being nuclear war and the Wolf Man). I remember sitting in the waiting room of Dr. Zyrill's office one day and hearing the bloodcurdling screams of a young dog-bite victim getting the first of his rabies' shot. This was just the beginning of a treatment requiring a series of some fifty or sixty injections smack in the belly button with a twenty-four-inch needle, or so I was led to believe by that most authoritative of school-yard sources—a sixth grader. And there I was at the edge of the Woods, strapped to a chair, with only an accordion to protect me; I, Orpheus, serenading the wild animals...with "Carnival of Venice." It must be true what they say about music soothing the savage beast, because none of the denizens of the Woods ever came near me, and, you know, sometimes the cats would serenade me back.

Before I was moved to the back of the backyard, I expressed some serious concerns to the folks. "What if it rains?" I pleaded. The old man was ready for that. He had rigged a golf umbrella to the chair and, while he was at it, attached a cup holder, too, so that my mom could supply me with plenty of Bosco to make chocolate milk on the drier warmer days. "It's an all-season studio, kiddo," he'd say.

"But what about lightning?" I worried.

"Don't give it a second thought," he told me. "There isn't much metal on you—or the accordion."

Then my mother would chime in that if they were ever to hear thunder, they'd be right out to fetch me. "At the first commercial," added the old man.

And so it was that this little spot of Jersey wilderness had become my musical sanctuary. For a long time things remained pretty much the same, rain or shine. It got so that I could play "Carnival of Venice" by heart. Mostly. But more and more, I was finding that my half-hour practice sessions seemed to be lasting a little longer than thirty minutes. (That I had never been given a watch for my birthday now began to take on the sinister aspect of a small piece of a much larger evil plot.) My parents would get busy with one thing or another and not remember to come out and liberate me from my chair. For a while I tried shouting, but all that accomplished was to stir the neighborhood dogs.

I ask you, what recourse did I have but to grow resentful? Okay, maybe it was more peaceful in the house without me around to pick fights with my brothers. Maybe there was less bickering over what program we would watch on our Philco TV set. And maybe there would be more of Mr. D's frozen "Wonder Bar D-Lights" to go around without me! And then I thought: *Wait a minute; maybe my mother and father had secretly wanted only two children all along!* Maybe This Whole Accordion Thing Was Their Big Chance! MAYBE I WOULD BE EATEN ALIVE BY RABID SQUIRRELS, MY REMAINS LEFT UNDISCOVERED FOR YEARS TO COME—exactly what they had in mind from the very start!

Suddenly I understood. It had all become as clear as day (although the air quality in Elizabeth, New Jersey, often undermined that particular expression). I had been Forsaken. Forgotten. Foredoomed! The edge of the Woods might well have been the end of civilization itself—an Antarctic ice floe, a desert island, another planet in an alternate universe because I was Alone, utterly alone in all the world...and I was Unloved.

Waiting to be unfettered, I began to imagine elaborate scenarios in which I was abducted by a UFO—accordion, chair, and all sucked up into the spaceship by an alien tractor beam, leaving my parents behind to live with the guilt and regret of having abandoned me to this fate through their heartless neglect. Sometimes I envisioned running away to join a carnival. In Venice!

There I'd run a Guess Your Age booth, make a fortune, then rent Carnegie Hall for an accordion recital, and *not* invite my family! My ultimate revenge fantasy involved getting struck by a bolt of lightning, which instead of frying my brain, transformed me into a superhero, not unlike what had happened to police scientist Barry Allen in the freak accident that made him the Flash. He was one of my favorite comic-book heroes, partly because we shared the same first name, but mostly because his superspeed powers were so unquestionably cool. Given the Flash's uncanny abilities, tied to a chair I could simply "vibrate" myself loose. Not to mention practice all of my music lessons in no more than two seconds flat.

As the days passed, I found myself spending less and less time concentrating on my accordion and more and more on concocting intricate fantasies. It soon became evident to me what my parents (and neighbors) had realized long before—that the money being spent on my weekly lessons could likely be put to better use. The "Carnival of Venice," by way of Elizabeth, was over.

Ultimately, the folks were pretty good about the whole thing. My mom made some excuse about needing her dish towels back. Oh, and the chair would prove useful, too. After all, Pop noted, Uncle Al would surely soon be visiting—"he just finished the *Mona Lisa.*" So one fateful afternoon, after I carefully packed the instrument in its big blue suitcase, the old man helped me lug it up to the attic—that final repository of outgrown toys, broken furniture, and now, finally, discarded dreams.

When I think back on those solitary accordion days, I know that no amount of practice would have made me anything remotely resembling a musical prodigy. Nor would I have grown up to become the next Yehudi Menuhin or even Benny Goodman. But I don't regret a single minute of all those hours strapped to a squeeze box in my backyard. While I was fixed firmly to that chair, my imagination was invited to run wild and free, and it took me everywhere—beyond Berwick Street and New Jersey and France and Mars, to places that never were and would never be…until put down on a piece of paper.

These days, as I sit at the keyboard instead of the buttons and keys, I always do so with a song in my heart. And, yes, sometimes—just sometimes—it's "Carnival of Venice." Yeah, I once played the accordion. Maybe that's why I'm a writer.

THE CONTRIBUTORS AND THEIR WORK

JAIME ADOFF's first book was a poetry collection called *The Song Shoots Out of My Mouth: A Celebration of Music*. It was named a Lee Bennett Hopkins Poetry Award Honor Book, an IRA Notable Book, and a New York Public Library Book for the Teen Age. His first young-adult novel, *Names Will Never Hurt Me*, was also cited as a New York Public Library Book for the Teen Age. His latest novel for young readers is *Jimi & Me*. He is the son of the late Newbery Award-winning author Virginia Hamilton and the renowned poet Arnold Adoff. Visit Jaime's Web site at www.jaimeadoff.com.

About "Twelve"

"I was listening to some old-school rap music and was inspired by the grooves and message. I kept the beats in my head and let my fingers run free over the keyboard. Before I knew it, 'Twelve' was born."

 **SANDY ASHER** is the author of twenty books for young readers, more than three dozen plays, and over two hundred articles, stories, and poems published in magazines. Her most recent release is a picture book, *Too Many Frogs!* She is also the editor of five collections of fiction, including *On Her Way: Stories and Poems About Growing Up Girl* and *With All My Heart, With All My Mind: 13 Stories About Growing Up Jewish*—winner of the 1999 National Jewish Book Award in children's literature. Sandy has also been honored with the American Alliance for Theatre and Education's Charlotte Chorpenning Award for a distinguished body of work in theater for young audiences, a National Endowment for the Arts fellowship grant, and an Aurand Harris Playwriting Fellowship from the Children's Theatre Foundation of America. She lives in Lancaster, Pennsylvania, with husband, Harvey; dog, Rudy; and cats, Natasha and Stanley. Visit Sandy's Web site at http://usawrites4kids.drury.edu/authors/asher.

About "Oh, Brother"
"I was—and still am—the younger sibling in our family, so I've felt all the feelings in my poem. My brother, Bob, is

eight years older than I am. When I began first grade, he was starting high school. When I started high school, he had finished college. I admired him from afar; he barely noticed me—except for teasing and the occasional fight. But, eventually, I did 'catch up,' and now we're good friends."

RAYMOND BIAL is the author and photo-illustrator of more than eighty books, including *Amish Home, The Underground Railroad, Where Lincoln Walked, One-Room*  *School, Ghost Towns of the American West,* and *Tenement: Immigrant Life on the Lower East Side.* He has published two collections of mystery fiction for children: *The Fresh Grave and Other Ghostly Stories* and *The Ghost of Honeymoon Creek.* He is currently working on "Lifeways," a series of books about Native American peoples. His books have received awards from the American Library Association, Children's Book Council, and many other organizations. He lives with his wife, Linda, and children, Sarah and Luke, in Urbana, Illinois. His daughter Anna is a fashion designer in New York City. To learn more about Raymond Bial and his work, readers may wish to visit his Web site: www.raybial.com.

About "Bucking Bales"
"I encountered Harry Proctor at a key moment in my youth. My voice had deepened and I had gotten my growth, but I

wondered what kind of man I would become. I discovered that Harry was not only strong and hardworking, but kind and cheerful. 'Bucking Bales' is a tribute to this exemplary man. Over the years, I came to be inspired by others, especially coaches and teachers. None were sports stars or celebrities, but individuals of exceptional character who were otherwise unassuming people—everyday heroes like Harry, who was as humble as the earth itself."

 **CLYDE ROBERT BULLA** was born on a farm near King City, Missouri. He went to a one-room country school and soon was writing his own stories and verses. When Clyde was twenty years old, he sold his first story. Later, he moved to town and worked on a newspaper, writing and publishing stories in his spare time. A teacher friend suggested Clyde write for children. *The Donkey Cart* was his first published children's book. He has since published more than eighty books for young readers, including *The Chalk Box Kid, Shoeshine Girl, A Lion to Guard Us*, and his autobiography, *A Grain of Wheat*. After fifty years of living and writing in California, he returned to his native state and now lives in Warrensburg, Missouri. Visit Clyde's Web page at http://usawrites4kids.drury.edu/authors/bulla.

* * *

About "The Chinese Boy"

"The school in the story was my own school in northern Missouri, where I went in the 1920s. It is long gone now. I dreamed of going to all the places in my big Frye & Atwood geography book and on the world globe we had, and I have been to most of them."

SNEED B. COLLARD III is a biologist, world traveler, speaker, and author of more than fifty books for young people, including *The Prairie Builders*; *A Platypus, Probably*; *Beaks!*; and *The Deep-Sea Floor*—all Junior Library Guild selections. He graduated from the University of California at Berkeley and also holds a master's degree from the University of California, Santa Barbara. He now resides in Missoula, Montana, and is the recipient of the *Washington Post*–Children's Book Guild Award for Non-fiction for his writing achievements. His first novel, *Dog Sense*, was inspired by his brilliant Frisbee-catching border collie, Mattie. His second novel, *Fire Birds*, will be released in late 2006 or early 2007.

Visit Sneed's Web site at www.sneedbcollardiii.com.

About "The Tower"

"When I was nine years old, I came face-to-face with the diving tower at Wakulla Springs. Although this story is fiction, most of the events actually did happen to me. Since my first glimpse of the tower thirty-seven years ago, I've visited Wakulla Springs at least eight or ten times. And every time I go, I have to meet that tower face-to-face. Even sitting here writing this, I can feel my adrenaline pump up imagining standing on top of it, looking down at the water swirling far below. Over the years, I got a crack at that thirty-five-foot platform many times. Sometimes the tower beat me. Other times, I overcame my fears and, at least temporarily, conquered the tower."

 Though he contributed a short story to *Dude!*, **BILL C. DAVIS** is the author of many award-winning plays for adults. His works have been performed all over the world: New York, Paris, Rome, Poland, Brazil, Argentina, Sweden, South Africa, Australia, and Germany. One of his plays, *Mass Appeal*, was made into a movie starring Jack Lemmon. While he was growing up, Bill came under the influence of his Irish aunt, uncles, grandmother, and great-grandmother. They were fierce, emotional, and poetic people. Now Bill works on his writing every day, and says he writes whatever he is moved to write. He looks forward to seeing his plays interpreted and performed in new ways. You can learn more about Bill C. Davis and his work on his Web site, www.billcdavis.com.

About "Family Meeting"

"In response to the question 'How did you find out about your brother's suicide?' I heard a boy say 'We had a family meeting.' And I went from there."

EDWIN ENDLICH's play *Bunked* pre-miered at the Sleepy Lion Theatre in Beverly, Massachusetts, and was subsequently awarded the 2002 Unpublished Play Reading Project National Award by the American Alliance for Theatre and Education. His plays *Ramp*, *3 Dirty Words*, and *Palace Grove* have also premiered at Sleepy Lion. His first play, *Without a View*, about his struggle with a speech disorder, premiered in 1997 in Connecticut. At age twenty, Edwin was the youngest presenter ever at the National Stuttering Association's Conference, where he addressed the issues of Drama Therapy and Psychodrama. A graduate of Emerson College, he currently lives in New York City.

About "To Speak or Not to Speak"

"I wrote 'To Speak or Not to Speak' so that guys would know that no one is perfect, and that we all fight to be normal sometimes."

JOSÉ CRUZ GONZÁLEZ has written many plays for young people, including *Tomás and the Library Lady, Thaddeus & 'Tila, Earth Songs, Old Jake's Skirts, Lily Plants a Garden, Two Donuts, Salt & Pepper, The Highest Heaven,* and *Marisol's Christmas.* He is a recipient of a 2004 Theatre Communications Guild/Pew National Theatre Residency grant and the American Alliance for Theatre and Education's Charlotte Chorpenning Award for a distinguished body of work in children's theater. He teaches theater at California State University, Los Angeles, and is a member of the Dramatists Guild of America and an Associate Artist with Cornerstone Theater Company and Childsplay.

About "Watermelon Kisses"
"As a boy, I remember sitting on our porch steps during hot summers eating sliced watermelons with my older brother. He used to play a lot of cruel tricks on my younger brothers and me. I also remember stories that my wife told me about her childhood, so I decided to combine our stories into 'Watermelon Kisses.'"

Christopher Medal winner **DAVID L. HARRISON**'s poems and stories have been widely recognized, anthologized, and translated into a dozen languages. Total sales of his seventy books exceed fifteen million copies. David's poems have been set to music and performed. *Somebody Catch My Homework*, Sandy Asher's play inspired by  his poetry, has been produced in the United States and abroad. David's work has been presented on television and radio and released on cassette and CD-ROM. His poem "My Book" is sandblasted into the Children's Garden sidewalk at Phoenix's Burton Barr Central Library. He wrote and coproduced a ninety-minute television documentary that was placed in the Library of Congress's collection for works of distinction. David has been a musician, scientist, editor, and businessman. He holds degrees from Drury, Emory, and Missouri State universities. He lives with his wife, Sandy, in Springfield, Missouri. In 1982, David was named poet laureate of Drury University.

You can visit David L. Harrison's Web page at http://usawrites4kids.drury.edu/authors/harrison.

About *"Take It from Me, Kid"*

"When I was a little boy, the world could be an exciting place, especially when gifts were involved. Those occasions meant candy. Rings with secret codes. Toy soldiers, water pistols, games in boxes that smelled like fun. Getting older was even better. Big boys got a whole string of firsts: Schwinn bicycle, Red Rider BB gun, bow and arrow, sleeping bag, pup tent, chemistry set. Ah, those were the days! Then came the year when toys were suspiciously absent. The boxes were all flat and professionally wrapped. They could only have come from one kind of store. They could only contain the sort of stuff my dad always got—shirts, pants, socks, underwear. I was doomed. I wasn't a little kid anymore. I was growing up and had the clothes to prove it. Some things you never forget. You have to write about them. You have to warn others."

RON KOERTGE taught at a community college in California for thirty-seven years before retiring to write full-time and to (not full-time, though) bet on racehorses. Two of his books have racetracks in them: *The Arizona Kid* and *Mariposa Blues.* Any reader interested in both poetry and baseball might like *Shakespeare Bats Cleanup,* while *Tiger, Tiger, Burning Bright* plops a live tiger in central California just to see what might happen. Ron lives in South Pasadena, California, with his wife, Bianca, and a middle-aged cat named Lily.

About "Lanky Boys with Cars"
"I like a challenge as much as the next guy, so when I saw that I could write a play for this anthology rather than a short story, I thought I'd give it a whirl. I see a handful of

plays every year, since a pal of mine works for South Coast Repertory in Orange County. And they appeal to me, since I write dialogue pretty well and plays are almost nothing but dialogue. The idea of being able to just have kids talk made me want to see if I could do it. The first draft wasn't very good, but there were a few good lines, and those made me want to write more."

BARRY KORNHAUSER is playwright-in-residence at the Fulton Opera House in Lancaster, Pennsylvania. His plays, which include *Cyrano, Power Play,* and *This Is Not a*  *Pipe Dream*, among others, have been performed at the Kennedy Center, the Shakespeare Theatre, and the Tony Award–winning Children's Theatre Company. Barry has been honored with the AATE Distinguished Play Award, the Bonderman Playwriting Prize, an ASSITEJ International Observership, the Helen Hayes Outstanding Play Award, and many grants and fellowships. Having given up on music, he instead practices daily at being a father to Max, Sam, and Ariel, fine musicians all. This is Barry's first short story.

About "The Ten-Ton Accordion"
"Not long ago my mother sent me a videotape comprising all of the eight-millimeter home movies that had been

taken of my brothers and me growing up. Popping it into the VCR, I was shocked to see myself tied to my old accordion with dish towels. The images brought back a flood of memories. Corrupted a bit by time and embellishment, I've shared these in 'The Ten-Ton Accordion.' The video also reminded me that as a struggling young adult—no longer strapped to a squeeze box, but very much strapped for money—I reluctantly sold my beautiful accordion for thirty-five dollars, proving me to be an even worse businessman than musician."

 **LIAM KUHN** is twenty-six years old. He writes stories and plays for children and adults and has received the Eleanor Frost Playwriting Prize, the Sidney Cox Memorial Prize for fiction, and the Richard Eberhart Literary Award. He has studied writing at Dartmouth College in New Hampshire and the National University of Ireland in Galway. Liam enjoys playing baseball and reading books. He lives in New Jersey with his family and his dog, Kiwi.

About "Heroes and Villains"
"I wrote 'Heroes and Villains' shortly after my father died. It was a difficult time for me, and writing the story was one of the things that helped me cope with the new emo-

tions I felt and the challenges I faced. Whenever I think about my dad, I remember how much he loved his family and how much of himself he sacrificed to protect, provide, and care for us. The father in 'Heroes and Villains' is a lot like my dad—he works hard all the time to make the world a better place for his family. In so many ways, my father was a superhero, even if he never wore a mask or cape."

JOSEPH ROBINETTE is the author or co-author of forty-nine published plays and musicals. He wrote the authorized stage adaptations of E. B. White's *Charlotte's*  *Web* and *Stuart Little* and C. S. Lewis's *The Lion, the Witch and the Wardrobe.* He also wrote the musical version of *Charlotte's Web* with composer Charles Strouse. Joe has won several national awards, including the Charlotte Chorpenning Cup for his body of work for young audiences and the American Alliance for Theatre and Education's Distinguished Play Award for his adaptation of Patricia MacLachlan's *Sarah, Plain and Tall.* He also received the Lindback Distinguished Teaching Award for "Demonstrated Excellence in the College Classroom."

About "Class Trip"
"A few years ago, my wife and I went to Baltimore. Our hotel room, to my delight, overlooked Camden Yard, home

of the Baltimore Orioles. (I've always loved baseball, and in my senior year of high school, I led my team in batting!) I could see home plate from our window, and I started thinking, What if a batter could hit a ball so hard that it...? Well, our hotel was too far away, and our room much too high, for a baseball to possibly reach the window. But I began to think... if the hotel were a little closer to Camden Yard and the room a bit lower, could it happen? And just like that, the idea for 'Class Trip' began to take shape."

BARBARA ROBINSON considers herself "a lucky author." The Herdmans—Ralph, Imogene, Leroy, Claude, Ollie, and Gladys—came into her head and onto her typewriter almost twenty-five years ago in *The Best Christmas Pageant Ever.* The Herdmans, she says, would be amazed to know that those books, and therefore their adventures, have received awards voted by children in many states and have been published all over the world. There are even Herdmans in Iceland!

You can visit Barbara Robinson on the Web at http:// usawrites4kids.drury.edu/authors/robinson.

* * *

About "A Pet for Calvin"

"My grandson Tomas briefly adopted a worm, and was asked by his mother whether he would want to be shut up in such a small space. He said no, "but I might like a sleep-over." That sentence didn't make it into the story, but it was that sentence that sparked my authorly instincts."

When **WALTER SIMONSON** was four years old, he became very sick. To help pass the time as he lay in bed, his mother gave him pencils and paper so he could draw pictures. He drew pictures that told stories, and he's loved drawing and telling stories ever since. After he grew up, he decided to write and draw picture stories in comic books. He's written and drawn many comics, including *Superman*, *Batman*, *Wonder Woman*, *Thor*, *X-Men*, *Fantastic Four*, *The Hulk*, *Battlestar Galactica*, and *Star Wars*. "The Squids" is his first prose story.

About "The Squids"

"Around Christmastime each year, the mall near my home fills up with little kiosks selling holiday shoppers everything from radio-controlled toy cars to Celtic jewelry to puffy slippers. One kiosk I saw as I was walking by was selling head massagers. The things had a creepy look about them, almost as though they were small metallic aliens. That was where my story began."

 **JOHN URQUHART** is an award-winning playwright whose plays for children are produced throughout the United States. He currently lives in Portland, Maine, with his wife, three children, and a dog named Ollie. He has written plays about skateboarders (*Operation Ollie: A Story of Skaters at War*), the challenges faced by children of immigrant refugees (*Lion Hunting on Munjoy Hill*), and most recently he adapted Karen Hesse's book *Witness* for the theater. When he isn't writing, he likes to go hiking and canoeing. He also likes to build tree forts and fish for trout.

About "The Enemy"

"An earlier version of 'The Enemy' was produced as part of Kentucky Scrapbook in 1988 by the Lexington Children's Theatre, Lexington, Kentucky. I wrote the first version of the play while living in Kentucky, a border state where families, friends, and communities were divided by the War Between the States. While researching the history of the American Civil War for this play, I was reminded of my own childhood, when my friends and I would play war and argue about who would play the Yankees and who would play the Rebels. Most of us wanted to be

Confederate soldiers, even though they had lost the war."

JANE YOLEN has written over 270 books.
Close to fifty of those are middle-grade
and young-adult novels, including the first
of the Rock 'n' Roll Fairy Tale books, *Pay the
Piper*, and *Boots and the Seven Leaguers: A Rock-and-Troll
Novel*. She is the author of the prizewinning Pit Dragon
Trilogy, and is working on a fourth book in the series. Her
novel *The Devil's Arithmetic* was made into a TV movie
starring Kirsten Dunst. Her collection of folktales particularly for boys is called *Mightier Than the Sword*. Jane Yolen's
books and stories have won (among many other awards)
two Nebulas, a Caldecott Medal, two Christopher Medals, a
World Fantasy Award, three Mythopoeic Fantasy Awards,
and the Jewish Book Award.

Her Web site is: www.janeyolen.com.

About "Going for Gold"
"What inspired the poem? Watching Michael Phelps win so
many Olympic swimming medals. I tried to imagine myself
as a kid being inspired by his feat. And while I can swim, I
sure can't swim like that!"

RICHARD ALAN YOUNG grew up in Fort Worth and
Abilene, Texas, and in Quito, Ecuador, in South America.

He graduated from the University of Arkansas at Fayetteville. He taught high school for twenty-five years, has worked thirty summer seasons at Silver Dollar City historic theme park, and has cowritten nine books with his wife, Judy. His work has received awards from Parents' Choice, *Storytelling World*, and *American Bookseller* Pick of the Lists. His books include *Favorite Scary Stories of American Children*, *African-American Folktales*, and *Race with Buffalo*.

Visit Richard and Judy Young's Web site at: www.yawp.com/stories.

About "The Marooned Boy"

"My father, who was one-eighth Seneca Indian, told and read to me Indian stories when I was a boy. This Caddo story has become the one I tell most often when performing for elementary-school kids."